Shoes to Fill

A

Mt. Hope Southern Adventure

Book Two

Lynne Gentry

TRAVEL LIGHT PRESS

Shoes to Fill (Mt. Hope Southern Adventures, Book Two)

Copyright © 2017 by Lynne Gentry

All rights reserved.

For bonus information visit: www.lynnegentry.com

This is a work of fiction. Names, characters, organizations, places, events, and incidents are either products of the author's imagination or are used factiously.

Cover photo © 2016 Lynne Gentry

Full Cover Design by Castle Creations

Edited by Gina Calvert

ISBN: 978-0-9986412-1-8

Summary

The highly-educated millennial, David Harper, is adrift.
He is also the pastor's son.
Or he was, until his father dropped dead in the pulpit.
When David learns his widowed mother
is in danger of losing the roof over her head,
he surprises everyone,
most of all himself,
and steps in to fill his father's shoes.
David knows it won't be easy to dynamite
the small congregation into the twenty-first century,
but it's the tough little blonde who blows his world apart.

Return once again to the humor and drama
of the small Texas town of Mt. Hope.

Fast-paced humor. Tear-jerking candor. Heart-melting romance.

Escape into another delicious southern adventure.

MT. HOPE SOUTHERN ADVENTURES

Walking Shoes

Shoes to Fill

Dancing Shoes

Baby Shoes

Check out Lynne Gentry's

Sci-Fi/Time Travel Adventures

The Carthage Chronicles

Healer of Carthage

Return to Exile

Valley of Decision

A Perfect Fit

Shades of Surrender

For My Son

You are your father's son.

Shoes to Fill

CHAPTER ONE

David stood beside his mother at the sanctuary door of Mt. Hope Community Church. His sister had bailed, claiming someone needed to go home and check on Grandmother. Maddie had always hated the duty of shaking hands with the exiting members. David, on the other hand, believed someone had to stand by Momma in her grief. He was smiling, but his mind remained focused on his feet and the uncomfortable blisters his father's Sunday shoes had rubbed. In an unusually rash decision to jump in and preach in his father's place, he'd failed to consider how painful it would be to step into shoes he could never fill.

"Davy." Maxine Davis elbowed her way to the front of the line. Before he could back away, her long, diamond-clad fingers shot out from the sleeve of her fur coat and wrapped around his arm. "We're so blessed that you've decided to replace your dad in the pulpit."

Replace Dad?

He'd not preached this morning to replace his recently deceased father. He'd preached to keep the board from evicting his mother from the parsonage. David knew he was operating on borrowed time. Sooner or later, the board would have to fill the pulpit with a qualified pastor and when they did, Momma would have to move out of her church-owned home.

He smiled inwardly at the memory of purposely running off the first replacement minister candidate who'd been recruited for the job just days after his father's death. He should feel bad about bursting the bubble of the overly zealous Postiers. But he didn't. The horror tales he'd told them about living in the parsonage had been the perfect set up for the regular Sunday morning visit of the Story sisters. The young preaching candidate had nearly dropped his towel when he exited the parsonage bathroom and found two old women intent on investigating his privacy. Ted Postier had barely taken the time to dry off before he loaded his family into David's grandmother's limo and begged Melvin to drive them to the nearest airport.

His mother had gotten on to him for exaggerating the tribulations of living in the parsonage, but, David reasoned, he'd actually saved the young couple from drying up in the

West Texas heat. Once his mother was emotionally strong enough to move on, the elder board could hire whomever they pleased. He would wish the new guy good luck, then he, too, would move on and sort out his own life … a task he'd put off far too long.

"Dad wouldn't want to leave anyone in a lurch." David couldn't pry himself from Maxine's claws. "I'm happy to fill in until things get settled."

"You're every bit as good as your father." Maxine tightened her grip as her gaze slid over to Momma. "Maybe even better."

David shook his head. "Dad was the real deal."

"Nobody could quote scripture like J.D. Harper," Maxine agreed. "But we are in desperate need of a theologian. Someone who can really dig deep." She squeezed his hand a little tighter. "You're not going back to Oxford, right?"

He would never get used to everyone knowing his business. "Not for now."

"And what about taking over your grandfather's law firm?" Maxine glanced at Leona. "Your mother's made it clear that's what she intends for your boy."

"The firm will be there when David is ready." Momma's undying support deserved more than the Band-Aid sermon he'd offered this morning.

"Well, in that case." Maxine's free hand reached behind her and, in a magician-like-slight-of-hand, produced her daughter.

"Nellie?" David's aversion to this particular redhead curdled his gut. How could he have missed his old nemesis in the sparse crowd?

"I texted Cornelia when I saw you in the pulpit. Said she should get here fast as she could. Told her of course you'd remember her," Maxine gushed. "After all, the preacher's son and the elder's daughter were practically inseparable growing up."

David's memories of Nellie were more like teenage nightmares. She'd hounded him all through junior high and high school. When they were in ninth grade she took her stalking to a new level and tricked him into following her into the baptistry changing room where she'd previously removed the light bulb. He'd never forget how she'd pressed him against the wall and planted a wet kiss on his ear. In his frantic attempt to escape, her braces snagged his neck and removed a layer of skin. Momma seemed to believe his explanation that he'd cut himself trying out his father's razor, but from then on she'd made it her business to make sure he and Nellie were never alone.

"Of course he remembers Nellie, Maxine." Momma

intercepted Maxine's attempt to put them together now. Once again, his mother had his back. Which was why it was his turn to have hers. "Don't you, David?"

"Uh, sure." David had no choice but to accept Nellie's outstretch hand. "It's been awhile, Nellie."

Nellie's eyes glowed with the same fiery intensity they had in that dark changing room. "Cornelia."

"Sorry," David mumbled, fuming that he had to stand here and pretend he was comfortable with the daughter of the chairman of the church board. "Cornelia."

"You're more handsome than I remember," Nellie purred, her gaze slithering down his neck. Though she managed to look demure enough for the church foyer, he could've sworn she was checking to see if her braces had left a scar. "And you're taller than you look on Facebook," she smiled at David's increasing discomfort. "I'm friends with your sister."

Furious that Maddie had posted anything that could aid Nellie's ability to stalk him again, he pulled free. "It's the shoes."

Nellie's eyes flitted to his feet. She frowned. "Why are you wearing Reverend Harper's old Sunday shoes?"

"For me," Momma interjected. "He did it for me."

"Davy always has been such a thoughtful young man," Maxine cooed. "And you must have worn those *new* shoes for

Davy, Leona." She pointed at the large red bows wrapping Momma's ankles.

Momma raised her chin. "I wore them for me, Maxine."

Maxine's nostrils flared. Before she could speak, Nellie broke in.

"I'm sorry I missed your sermon, David." Nellie flashed her expensive smile again. "Traffic was horribly slow because of the icy roads." She still had those cat-like green eyes he didn't trust, but he wasn't a stupid kid anymore either. People change. Nellie had grown up, that was for sure. She was tall. Dark auburn hair. Attractive. Maybe she'd also outgrown her crush on him. Maybe the sparks were only flying in his imagination. "We should get together," she continued. "Catch up." Nellie walked her fingers up his jacket lapel. "Reconnect."

Or maybe not.

"I'm planning on keeping him pretty busy, Cornelia," Momma chirped. "But maybe you two can *catch up* at the New Year's Eve party. Oh, excuse me. There's Bette Bob." Momma gently moved Maxine and Nellie aside and reached for the next member in line. "Let me hug that dear, sweet niece of yours, Bette Bob." Momma wrapped her arms around Amy. "I can't thank you enough for all you've done for my family." She leaned back and said, "Can we, David?"

"No. I mean, yes, thanks." David offered his hand to the

attractive blonde in a pretty pink sweater. "Grandmother told us your care is the reason she's not suing the hospital for sending her to the nursing home rehab."

Amy's firm but brief handshake was a jolt to his entire system. "Then I did my job." She withdrew her hand and turned her attention directly to his mother. "Mrs. Worthington feeling better since her rehab release?"

"She was thrown out," Momma said, bluntly.

David couldn't believe his mother's candor. He'd never seen her risk telling anyone anything that might tarnish the perfect image she'd always strived to uphold. Especially not a member of the church. What other changes could he expect if he didn't help her hold it together?

"When does she start her in-home therapy?" Amy asked, still ignoring David.

"Monday," David interjected.

Amy's genuinely pleased smile disappeared. "Tell her to do what the therapists advise and she'll be back on her feet in no time." She spun and headed for the fellowship hall exit.

David watched Amy's blonde's curls swish across her perfect shoulders. He was sick and tired of people feeling like they could treat the preacher's kids as if they didn't have feelings. Granted, they'd clashed over a plate of fudge at his father's funeral lunch, but that didn't give her the right to continue to blow him off. Of course, he hadn't exactly been at his best that day, but then he had just buried his father. Tempting as it was to claim he deserved a break, he regretted that he'd acted like a jerk. If he was going to stick around for the next year, he couldn't avoid someone who seemed committed to turning up every Sunday.

"Excuse me, Momma." David pushed past Bette Bob and chased after the quick stepping nurse. "Amy!" His shout bounced off the wooden pews in the empty sanctuary. "Wait up."

She kept going.

He exceeded her hurried stride until he overtook her. "Hey." David snagged her arm. "I just want to apolo—"

Amy wheeled and faced him head on. "So this is your plan?"

"Excuse me?"

She looked at his fingers digging into her soft, pale sweater. "You preached about how your father wanted this church to grow. To be effective in changing this community, and possibly the world. You said if we all pulled together, Mt. Hope Community Church could have a bright future. Do you really believe that?" Challenge blazed in her stunning blue eyes.

He dropped his planned apology and seized the challenge.

"I know it's not going to be easy, but, yes, I do."

"Does that mean you're going to lead the charge?"

"You sure you don't have a legal background? You're killer on the cross-examination."

"Is strong-arming the method you intend to employ?" Her eyes cut once again to his hold on her arm.

He let go. "Sorry." He didn't intend to spend every encounter apologizing. "You're right. I don't know anything about growing a church."

"I know."

David bristled at her unexpected honesty. "So you don't think I could turn this place around?"

"*Jesus* would have a hard time turning this place around."

"Is that a challenge?"

She sighed. "I don't want this church to close its doors, but my aunt told me she's worried that's exactly what will happen, especially now that the Harper era is over. It is over, right?"

"I don't—"

"Once you assuage your guilt, you'll take your mother and—"

"My guilt?"

"Something made you step into your father's pulpit today."

"What's that supposed to mean?"

"I don't think you preached because you've suddenly felt

called to pastor a small town church."

After all he'd endured these past few days, she'd hit too close to the battle in his soul. "Don't count me out." David wheeled and strode toward his mother.

His father's legacy hung in the balance. He would not let it, nor his mother, sink on his watch … and the beautiful blonde with the inexplicable chip on her shoulder could eat his dust.

CHAPTER TWO

Amy stormed into the fellowship hall, kicking herself for letting this man she barely knew have the last word. Again. What was it about him that set her off? It wasn't like her to let a guy get under her skin. Especially one who acted so certain of himself, but was obviously suffering from something deeper than grief. She dealt with people in pain all the time. It was her compassion that made her so good at her job. Where was her grace for this hurting soul? Her hand froze on the coffee pot plug. What if she was confusing her lack of compassion with too much empathy?

She knew how it felt to lose a parent. Three years ago a State Trooper's call had forever changed her life. Remembering that awful night now brought a fresh wave of tears. Amy swiped her cheeks. Apparently, the dark days weren't completely behind her. Maybe they never would be. She dug her phone from her purse. Her finger hovered over the play arrow on a voicemail she would never delete. A message she had memorized and wouldn't risk playing where others could hear. She let the message play in her head.

"It's one doctor's opinion, Amy," her dad said over Christmas music playing on his car radio. *"Don't swear off men just yet,"* her mom added with the same eternal optimism that had carried Amy through years of medical issues. *"We'll meet you at your dorm and make a plan,"* Dad promised. *"Love you, kiddo,"* they said together. *"See you soon."*

A minute later John and Libby Maxwell were dead, hit head-on by a driver skidding out of control on a patch of black ice.

Amy dropped the phone in her purse, the ache in her heart sharp as the day death dealt its blow. Adding David's loss to her own would not help her...or him, for that matter.

In nursing school the teachers had preached the merits of maintaining a professional distance, citing the risks of becoming too emotionally involved. Never once had any of her instructors added the stipulation that she should avoid handsome men in need of rescuing. After her parents died, she'd been forced to make the most painful of all decisions on her own. Better to keep all men at bay than risk having her heart broken if she fell in love with one who wanted children.

She should thank David for making her aware that this heightened sense of care she was feeling for him was simply strong empathy. Now that she knew what she was dealing with, she could dig her toes into the sand and safely toss him a life preserver without being dragged under.

Helping him deal with his grief was not only her responsibility as a medical professional, it was the Christian thing to do. Then why did she feel like such a coward?

Amy yanked the plug and ripped the filter holder from the industrial coffeepot tower. With an angry flick of her wrist she dumped the grounds in the trash.

"I thought I'd find you here." Aunt Bette Bob dropped her purse and Bible on the counter. "Ever since you were a little girl, the moment you got upset you'd go in search of something to clean. Libby Ann used to say she could always tell when something was bothering her Amy by—"

"The order in my room." Amy could never thank her aunt enough for trying to fill the void her parents left, but sometimes Aunt Bette Bob sounded so much like her mother it made the hole seem bigger. "The sooner we get this mess cleaned up, the sooner we can tackle that roast you put on this morning."

Aunt Bette Bob cocked her head, obviously not buying

Amy's attempt to dismiss her warring emotions. "I remember David's first sermon." She took a donut hole from the pastry box. "His father was so proud. He would have been even prouder today."

Amy ripped a paper towel from the roll and swiped the inside of the filter bowl. "I'm sorry I didn't have the chance to really get to know Reverend Harper."

"If David is even half the man his father was, Mt. Hope Community just might keep its doors open." Aunt Bette Bob popped the donut hole in her mouth and pointed a finger Amy's way while she chewed. "Any girl lucky enough to snag that fine young man would be blessed."

"Aunt Bette Bob, you know I can't go there—" Amy stopped mid-protest, her attention drawn to the stranger who'd just stepped through the back door of the fellowship hall. "Can I help you?"

A tall, young man tugged at the sparse red hairs on his chin. "Uh …" He stuffed reddened hands into the pockets of dirty jeans. A heavy backpack hung from his thin shoulders. A sour mix of neglected hygiene and stale campfire smoke drifted across the room. His breathing was labored, deep and gasping, like he'd been running for his life. He shuffled his muddy tennis shoes on the mat. "I'm thirsty." Shame tinged his ragged voice. "Was hopin' for uh … uh … "

"Water?" Aunt Bette Bob licked her fingers. "We've got that and a few left over donut holes." She snatched up the box and hurried toward him. "If this was the first Sunday of the month we'd have had a full spread of potluck here to share."

"This is more than I deserve." He took the box. "What day is it?"

"It's Sunday, son." Aunt Bette Bob called over her shoulder. "Amy, is there any coffee left in that pot?"

"I'll check." Amy snatched a Styrofoam cup from the cupboard and placed it under the spigot. The brew was stout but at least it was still hot. "Here you go." She set the cup on a table and pulled out a chair. "Sit. You look a little—"

The young man lifted a donut hole from the box and stared at it like it had been so long since he'd eaten he'd forgotten how. Before he got the sweet to his mouth, his hand began to shake. He grabbed his stomach. Donuts spilled across the floor. His eyes rolled back in his head and his knees buckled.

Amy lunged for the man collapsing in front of her. "Get help," she ordered.

While her aunt sped toward the sanctuary yelling at the top of her lungs, Amy lowered the unconscious man to the tile.

She kicked donut holes out of her way and crouched beside him. It took some effort to slide the heavy backpack from his arm.

David flew into the room. "Amy!" He rushed to her side and squatted. "You okay?"

"Yes."

"Should I call Maddie?"

"No! 9-1-1."

"Done." David pulled out his phone but he didn't leave her. "Juanita, this is David Harper. We need an ambulance at Mt. Hope Community. A man has collapsed." He moved the phone from his ear and asked, "Do you know his name?"

Amy loosened the zipper on the man's hoodie. "I've never seen him before."

"We don't know him," David told the dispatcher. "I'd guess him to be in his mid-twenties."

She pushed up his sleeve and searched for a pulse. "He looks younger to me."

David repeated Amy's report on her patient's vitals to the dispatcher of the only ambulance service in the county. "Charlie's on his way." He slid his phone in his suit pocket. "Anything I can do?"

By now, the fellowship hall had filled with David's mother, Maxine, Nellie, and the Story sisters.

"Keep them out of my way," she whispered to David.

"Sure." David stood and gently eased the women toward the kitchen. "Let's give Amy room to work." He ricocheted back to Amy's side and placed himself directly at her elbow. "Now what?"

"I meant you, too."

"Oh, right." He scrambled to his feet and buttoned his suit coat. "You're the professional."

As Amy worked to assess the unconscious man for possible injuries, she could feel everyone's eyes on her back, especially the dark eyes of the handsome man she'd pretty much called a loser.

Nola Gay craned her neck. "He looks familiar, don't you think, Sister?"

"You know a lot of vagrants, do you, Nola Gay?" Maxine pulled her daughter close.

"I think he may have escaped from the prison," Nola Gay said.

"He's not wearing a uniform." Etta May pointed out. "But he does resemble one of those shifty-eyed characters we've seen on the sketches at the post office."

"I bet that's where we've seen him, Sister," Nola Gay agreed. "We never forget a face, do we, Etta May?"

Amy forced herself to block out the ensuing argument between Maxine and the Story twins. By the time Charlie's ambulance screeched to a halt under the portico, the Story sisters had convinced Maxine the emaciated man was a convict on the run and they were lucky to be alive.

Charlie burst through the door dragging a squeaky gurney and his skinny son behind him. "Y'all are gettin' to be regulars," Charlie belted breathlessly.

"Charlie!" Amy tilted her head toward the pale-faced pastor's wife who was obviously reliving the recent loss of her husband in this same church building.

"Sorry, Leona," Charlie mumbled.

"Don't worry about me," Leona said. "This boy needs you now."

Charlie and his son lowered the stretcher beside the man. "What we got here, Amy?"

"His pulse is weak." Amy helped Charlie shift the patient onto the stretcher. "At a minimum he's dehydrated and malnourished."

"And most likely high." Charlie cinched the strap across the man's chest. "Hauled one of his kind out from under that new overpass just the other day."

David stepped forward. "His kind?"

"You know, homeless veterans." Charlie gave the gurney a tug. "I swear. That new highway bypass between here and the base may be killin' the local businesses but it draws vagrants to town like buzzards to roadkill." He used his broad backside to hit the door latch. "It's gettin' to be a real epidemic. The government's going to have to do something or we'll have to start lockin' our doors."

David picked up the stranger's pack and pushed between Amy and the gurney. "I think that's jumping to some pretty serious conclusions, Charlie."

Everyone scampered out to watch like a bunch of rubberneckers.

Charlie heaved the gurney over the curb. "My sister lives on the edge of town and it's all she can do to keep the vagrants out of her henhouse."

"Do you have proof this guy has been stealing chickens?" David's adamant defense of the stranger surprised Amy.

Charlie pulled a feather off the patient's sweatshirt. "I ain't no detective, but I don't think your friend here's been eatin' pigeons."

"He's not our friend!" Maxine shouted.

Amy couldn't contain her growing exasperation. "If this boy doesn't get to the hospital STAT it won't matter what he's done to stay alive." She took the backpack from David. "I'll ride with him."

Charlie shrugged. "Kid smells like a henhouse."

"I've smelled worse." Amy climbed in and began to loosen the belts Charlie had cinched way too tight. Right before Charlie closed the door, she looked up to see David standing on the sidewalk, a scowl on his face. She hated to ask for help, but her car was a standard and her aunt refused to learn how to drive a stick. "Would you take my aunt home?"

David shook his head. "Momma can do it. I'm going to the base to see what kind of governmental assistance we can get this man. Text me his name, date of birth, and social, once he's conscious."

"Thank you," Amy said, more surprised than grateful.

"I may not know how to grow a church, but I can navigate legal red tape."

As Charlie closed the door on the interim preacher, Amy felt her heart burst wide open.

CHAPTER THREE

Momma undid the ankle straps on her uncharacteristically high red heels she'd finally had the courage to wear. "Charging in to save the underdog was your father's undoing."

David dropped his suit jacket on the couch. "Investigating whether or not a man is eligible for military benefits is hardly charging in." He undid his tie. "After I change, I'm going to head out to the base. Hopefully, Amy can get the guy's personal info by the time I get there." He pulled out his phone. "Shoot! I forgot to give her my number and I don't have hers."

"She gave me her cell number while your grandmother was in the hospital." Momma's smile was a little too pleased. "I'll forward it to you."

He tossed his tie over the arm of the couch. "Put the brakes on those matchmaking wheels, Momma."

"Amy Maxwell would be—"

"My helping this guy out has nothing to do with Amy Maxwell."

"What guy?" Maddie stood in the doorway wearing a robe and her hair in a towel.

"Didn't you hear the ambulance?"

"I was in the shower. There wasn't any hot water after the Postiers got finished this morning." Maddie looked between David and Momma, her keen sense of observation kicking in. "What did I miss?"

"A stranger passed out in the fellowship hall and Amy saved him," Momma explained.

"Why didn't you come get me?"

"You had to check on Grandmother, remember?" David didn't hold back his irritation that she'd left him to deal with the members of Mt. Hope Community, Amy Maxwell included.

Momma carefully removed her shoes. "David is going out to the base to see if the young man is military."

"David's diving into church work?" Maddie's brows rose. "The plot thickens."

He kicked off his father's shoes. "Helping a guy who's down on his luck is what Dad would have done."

"So you wear Dad's shoes, preach his sermon, and now you're him?" Maddie's teasing had an edge of warning he didn't appreciate.

"I didn't ask for your approval."

Momma stepped between them. "Maddie, would you mind taking your Grandmother her lunch?"

Maddie quickly considered the situation in that diagnostic way of hers, then said, "You've always had more than my approval, big brother. I've always had your back." She turned and left him to chew on the one thing he knew to be true. He could always count on his little sister to tell him the truth. Was he trying to be like Dad out of guilt or was it something deeper?

Momma patted the sofa. When she realized David was too worked up to sit, she started in on him anyway. "Defending the underdog has always appealed to you, David. I think it's why you love the law." She bent over and rubbed her foot with both hands. "But if you're going to take your father's place for a bit, I just don't want you to make the same mistakes we made."

"Momma, Dad was the saint. Not me."

Her head popped up. "Whatever made you believe your father was a saint? He had his shortcomings, and the church folks have been more than happy to point out mine."

"You see, that's where you and I are different. I don't care what the members at Mt. Hope Community Church think."

"Then you won't last two weeks."

"Thanks for the vote of confidence." Feeling guilty, David sat on the coffee table and faced his mother. "Momma, what exactly do you believe you and Dad did wrong?"

"Maybe we should have been more ..."

"Perfect?"

"Nobody wants to fail in this life, David." She looked at him with watery eyes. "Your father and I certainly never wanted to let the Lord down."

"And you think you did?"

"You saw the numbers today. What do you think?"

"Impact can't always be measured in numbers."

"I know you'll do things differently here, as you should, but is it wrong for a mother to want to spare her child the painful lessons she's endured?"

"Momma, this isn't a matter of me doing things differently." David took her hand. "I preached for *you* today. No one else."

"Me?"

"I didn't want you to suffer Maxine's barbs about the strain the empty pulpit was putting on her husband."

"But you told your grandmother you didn't want the firm."

"Just because practicing law doesn't appeal to me for now"—David softened his tone before finishing up his argument—"don't think that means I'm bucking to become a pastor forever."

"What *do* you want to do with your life?"

"I don't know."

She studied him for a moment, her eyes taking on that dreamy contented look that always made him wish he could actually live up to whatever it was she saw in him. "Maxine is right," she said quietly. "When it comes to skill in the pulpit, you *are* as good as your father." She silenced his protest with a gentle finger to his lips. "You know how much I loved listening to your father preach, but *you* may be even better."

"Maxine has her own agenda."

"Nellie?"

He gave her a don't-even-go-there look.

Thankfully, she didn't. Instead, she opted to change the subject. "Wayne Darling says a widow should wait a year after losing a loved one before making any drastic changes."

"That's good advice. You should take it."

"The Board isn't going to give me a year."

"Then that's another good reason for me to stay. Maddie's flying out in a couple of days for her residency interviews. But I can stay to make sure they do."

Momma leaned back with a sigh and he could tell she was gearing up for one of her now-son lectures. "Remember how I used to drill you and your sister about what to do if our van ever went over a bridge?"

This was not the tactic he was expecting. "Save Momma?"

She nodded. "Truth is, I knew you would have jumped in for me no matter what. You know how I knew this?"

He shook his head. "No, and I don't see what your water phobia has to do with the vagrant in the fellowship hall."

"Beneath your tough-guy exterior beats a heart that longs to save others. David, you've been a rock for me these past few weeks, but it's not your job to see me settled."

"Maybe not, but I can keep Maxine and the Board from throwing you out on the streets."

"How?"

"I can fill Dad's pulpit for a year."

Understanding brought her forward immediately. "My dear sweet boy, I'm not going to let you waste a year of your life sitting around here doing something you hate."

"I didn't say I hated preaching. I just don't know if a lifetime of doing it twenty-four-seven is for me."

"David, even if your heart's greatest desire was to preach, you can't just take your father's pulpit. The pastor must be Board-approved and voted in by a majority of the congregation."

"What if I could convince them to designate me interim pastor? They could keep me on for a pittance of what it would cost to hire someone else. Plus, they wouldn't have the lag time between interviewing and the actual arrival of a new hire. It wouldn't take very many weeks of Howard preaching to totally shut this place down."

"Maybe you should use that law license." Momma's tired grin did not reach her eyes. "Those are some pretty convincing arguments."

"It's a simple matter of economics…yours included."

"So filling your father's pulpit is your version of saving your drowning mother?"

"It's my version of making it up to Dad."

Momma swallowed. "The Board has never been in this situation before, so I'm not sure what they'll decide. Either way…"

"We're back to winning over Maxine."

She gave him a weary nod. "If I've learned anything these past few weeks, it's this: life is short. In a blink of an eye, it's thirty years later and you can find yourself stuck somewhere you never intended to be. Saddest of all, you're not even sure which misstep tripped you up." She clasped his hand. "Except in your case. I know, from experience, you're choosing a step that will put you on a very difficult path." She squeezed hard. "Your father forgave you a long time ago. It's time for you to forgive yourself."

"Momma, Dad would want me to take care of you. I want to take care of you, but I don't have any money. What I can do is help you sort the legalities of Dad's estate. While I do, you can save what you make at the newspaper and I can preach and help support you. A strong argument can be made for the financial benefits of the church not having to pay to relocate a new family. I'm sure the Board will see an interim plan as a win/win for everyone."

"Everyone but you."

David leaned forward and kissed her cheek. "Think of it as buying you that year you need before making any big changes." He left before the truth of what she was saying could change his mind.

CHAPTER FOUR

Amy hung another bag of fluid above her patient's head. "Need anything else, Mr. Freestone."

"Angus," he mumbled. "Mister Freestone was the trucker who knocked-up my mom."

"Can I call him for you?"

"You got a direct line to hell?" His glassy eyes slid her direction. "My old man drank a bottle of tequila, drove his rig over a cliff, and went down in a ball of flames."

"I'm sorry."

"Me and mom celebrated." He saw her flinch. "Should have spared you the ugly details. After all, you saved my life."

"Technically, the doc in the ER—"

He held up a limp palm. "I don't blame you for wondering whether or not I was worth saving."

"Angus—"

"No, really. I've wondered that myself."

"I believe you *are* worth my attention. And now that we know you have diabetes, I can help you learn how to manage it." Determined to make up for missing the obvious signs of DKA, Amy tried again. She, of all people, shouldn't have been fooled by his symptoms. She straightened the items on his bedside table. "I'll need to complete your medical history, but before we tackle those questions, do you have anyone who'd want to know you're sick?"

"Not a soul in this world, pretty lady."

"That seems so unfair."

He let his head loll toward the window. "Life ain't always fair."

She was in the middle of charting the boy's sketchy medical history when a soft knock at the door drew her attention. "Up to a visitor, Angus?" she asked her patient.

Angus closed his eyes. "Not really."

"I'll tell them to come back later." She left her computer and went to the door. "David?"

"Sorry it took so long." David's mussed hair looked as if he'd forgotten to look in a mirror after he'd hurriedly pulled a t-shirt over his head and thrown on his leather jacket. "Had to take a hatchet to all the governmental red tape."

While this casually dressed David appeared much more approachable than the suited man she'd tangled with after church, she was surprised by the warrior concealed beneath his thick skin. He'd gone to battle for someone less fortunate without a moment's hesitation. Yet, he was still noticeably anxious. Uneasy, like he'd been when she took him back to see his grandmother after her hip surgery. That day, she'd read the tension in his jaw as his aversion to hospitals, but now she wondered if the real culprit was an aversion to her.

The possibility that there were many things she'd misread about this man prickled her skin. "Have you eaten?"

"I'll grab something later." He shoved his hand in his jeans pockets. "How is he?"

She glanced over her shoulder. Angus gave her a hit-the-road thumb signal. Amy nodded toward the hall. "Come on, I'll buy you a cup of coffee." She took him to the coffee machine hidden in the small closet behind the nurse's station. She filled a cup. "Take anything in it?"

"Black's good."

Their fingers brushed when she handed off the cup.

A weary grin lifted the corner of his mouth. "Big spender."

"It's the least I could do after you spent the afternoon helping me help Angus." Close enough to worry that her racing heart could be heard within the confines of the small space, she covered by saying, "So, what did you find out?"

David swallowed a quick sip. "You sure his real name is Angus Freestone?"

"He doesn't have any ID on him so I guess we'll just have to take him at his word. Why?"

"According to the military, Angus Freestone never served."

"It was a long shot." She resisted the urge to rearrange the stray strand of hair that had fallen across David's forehead. "Thanks for trying."

"So what happens now?"

"First, we get him back on his feet."

"Drug rehab?"

"He's not an addict as far as we can tell."

"If you believe that, I can see why you also believe his name is Angus Freestone."

"Look, I screwed up. Okay?"

"Whoa. You lost me." Confusion knit David's brow. "I thought we were finally having a civil conversation."

"Breathing hard. Thirsty. Abdominal pain. I missed a life-threatening condition." Reciting the boy's obvious symptoms out loud made her feel even guiltier. "I assumed he was homeless because of illegal substance abuse. I judged him."

"We all did." He snagged her arm. "Wait a minute. How do you know he's not an addict?"

His hold wasn't anything like the angry grip he'd had on her after church. This time his fingers wrapped her in support, a sensation she hadn't felt since her parents died. "His blood and urine tests came back clean."

"So why was he acting all crazy?"

"DKA."

"You're going to have to help me out here, Amy."

"Diabetic Ketoacidosis. Confusion is one of the symptoms. No telling how long he's had episodes of stumbling around. He didn't even know he was diabetic."

"Then how were you supposed to know?"

"I should have caught his fruity breath."

"How? Kiss the guy?" His dislike of his own suggestion set her back.

"You don't get it." Her body quivered with pent-up emotions. "He could have died right there in the church." The moment the words came out of her mouth, David's expression sobered. "I'm sorry," she rushed on desperate to repair the damage. "I didn't mean to bring up … I wish I'd been there when your father had his heart attack. Maybe I could have done something for him and … today had to have been very rough for you and your mother."

"Don't beat yourself up." David emptied his coffee cup. "The man looked and smelled like roadkill. I didn't notice his breath either."

David Harper obviously didn't want to talk about his father. So noted.

She didn't know why she'd let herself cross such a dangerously personal line. Despite the support his touch lent her now, their previous encounters hadn't exactly forged a friendship. So why was she charging on, busting a gut to tell him everything? "In nursing school they test you on stuff like body odors. Today, I failed."

He chucked his empty cup in the trash. "Tomorrow you won't."

"How can you be so sure?"

His eyes locked with hers. "You strike me as the kind of woman who never makes the same mistake twice."

She stopped babbling like a crazy woman and stared at the guy who'd just seen something admirable in her. "I wish that were true."

"What do you mean?"

"I judged you, too. And I'm sorry."

"I had it coming, don't you think?" When she didn't respond, a teasing grin poked dimples into his cheeks. "C'mon, admit it."

"Sort of." Amy smiled in spite of how difficult he was making it for her to apologize. Her aunt was right. Deep down, the preacher's son was a decent guy. Why else would he put his whole life on hold to come home and help his mother? "I know how it feels to lose someone you love," she said softly.

His playfulness vanished behind the shadow that came over his face. "That's what everyone says."

She hadn't meant to sound trite. However, she wasn't willing to confess she'd seen herself in this man's reaction, would have taken the statement she'd just made in the very same way. She recognized his anger flare-ups for what they were, the identical protection mechanisms she still employed whenever the raw ache of her loss overtook her. Being rude kept people at a safe distance. Distant people did not have to be loved or trusted to stick around. If she didn't love, then she couldn't get hurt when they left her.

She took a breath. "I also know it takes a while before you're at your best again."

"Guess it's good to know I won't always feel like punching every patronizing …" David didn't finish his thought, obviously embarrassed that she might have thought he meant her. "I better let you finish your shift. Call if our friend Angus needs anything."

"David," she touched his arm. Every muscle in his arm tensed beneath her fingers but he did not pull away.

"You're not going to tell me it will get better, are you?" His doubtful tone struck something raw inside her.

"No one can promise that." She held out her right hand in one last attempt at a truce. "Thanks for everything."

This time he was the one who cut their physical contact short, as if the hum passing between their locked hands shocked him as much as it did her. "Hey, what are pastors for, right?"

David left her to chew on her earlier indictment of his inability to minister. She regretted goading him about the church. Saving Mt. Hope Community Church would take all of them working together. But that didn't mean the urge to brush the strand of hair from his dark chocolate eyes and tell him he wasn't alone should be her next order of business.

CHAPTER FIVE

"I thought I smelled coffee." Momma breezed into the kitchen, trailed by the dog. She opened the back door and Tater shot out into the yard. "Why are you up so early?"

David raked his hair. "Why are *you* so dressed up on a Monday?"

Momma took her favorite mug from the cupboard. "Modyne frowns on tardiness."

David cringed inside. Momma deserved his support. "I forgot you have to go to work today." He didn't know if he'd ever get used to his mother working at anything other than being a pastor's wife. On the other hand, she seemed comfortable in a jacket, skirt, and heels...almost as if she'd finally put on her real skin and he was proud of her. "I bet you're the best-dressed obit reporter this town has ever seen."

"Thanks." Momma's brows knit. "I think."

He'd mentally replayed his conversation with Amy a million times. He didn't need another degree to know his communication skills with women needed work. "No, I mean you look professional."

Momma smoothed her skirt. "I'm a little late to the employment game to call my new job at the Messenger a profession."

"Whatever you want to call this new adventure, it suits you, Momma."

She gave a little shrug. "Jury's still out on whether or not Ivan Tucker keeps me."

"Ivan knows a good thing when he sees it."

"Appreciate the vote of confidence." She patted his back on her way to the dishwasher just like she had so many times when he was a boy. "What's on your agenda today?" She retrieved a clean bowl.

He took a deep breath and braced himself. "I thought I'd go to the office."

Momma straightened and closed the dishwasher door with her hip. "What office?"

"Dad's."

"Oh." She stiffened and set the bowl on the counter. "Does this mean you intend to go through with your plan to take your father's place?"

He weighed the words he'd been practicing since four this morning. The last thing he wanted to do was to disappoint her if he changed his mind. "I want to try it."

She took his cheeks in her hands. "You don't have to do this for me, David."

"I have to do it for me."

Her eyes searched his. When she located his resolve, the stubborn streak she'd never been able to bend to her will, she kissed his forehead. "Since you insist on hanging around, I could use your help."

Finally, something to make him feel less like a heel and more like a man worthy of his mother's admiration. "Name it."

"You remember Saul Levy?"

"The JAG lawyer who used to come to church once in a while?"

"He traveled a lot until his wife died a couple of years ago. He's retired from the military and set up a private practice here in town."

"You're not trying to throw me off my plan and set me up to go into business with Saul, are you?"

She shook her head. "He called yesterday. Said I should get started on probating your father's will. I didn't even know your father had a will. I've made an appointment with him today and I'd like you to go with me."

"Dad didn't tell you he'd executed a will?"

"No." She pulled out the stool next to him and sat down. "It's so unlike your father to keep secrets."

"Maybe he wanted to make things easy as he could for you, which is what a will is for."

"I don't see how a will could make any of this easy."

David ran his finger around the rim of his cup. How had the man who never seemed fazed by living in a glass house kept such a big secret? And why would he? "Let's get Dad's affairs settled so we can plan the future."

She swallowed hard. "Settled sounds so…so final."

He understood her reluctance to close the door on things left unsaid. He would give anything for five minutes to apologize to his father. "Probate takes a while. We'll tell Saul to take it slow." He took the cereal box from her shaky hands. "Where can I find Dad's mystery attorney?"

"He's renovated the space above Dewey Hardware."

"When do I need to be there?"

"After lunch."

"Breathe, Momma." He squeezed her shoulder. "We can do this."

An hour later, David was showered and standing in the freezing wind swirling outside the door of the church office.

For the past five minutes, he'd been giving himself the same pep talk he'd given his mother with her cornflakes.

The intercom crackled.

"You comin' in or not, David?" Shirley's voice reminded him that perhaps he, too, wasn't quite ready for his father's departure to be final. And that's exactly what would happen the moment he stepped into his father's office and assumed his father's place.

He could do this. He had to do this. David blew into his cupped fists then gave a thumbs-up signal to the small security camera mounted under the eaves. A buzzer sounded.

"It's op—" Shirley cut out.

After a couple of deep breaths, David pulled on the unlocked door. He wiped his feet on the mat and followed the musty carpet toward the office complex.

Complex was a generous term, a term coined by the elder board and one they used lavishly in the pastor's job description they'd posted online. The first minister candidate, the one David had helped leave town in a hurry, had believed he was coming to work with a full-fledge staff. The complex was really nothing more than a cubby hole for Shirley, the antique church secretary; a small youth minister's office that had been empty since David was in middle school; and his father's office.

David adjusted the laptop bag cutting into his shoulder. "Hey, Shirley."

"James David Harper!" The silver-haired woman grabbing him in a big bear hug was the only person he allowed to call him by his full name. She let him go and pointed at the candy dish on her desk. "I've got a new stash of baby Snickers tucked away just for you." She'd bought his affections years ago with pieces of chocolate and he wasn't ashamed to let her keep making installments.

He lifted the lid to her crystal candy dish. "I think we are going to work together just fine, Miss Shirley."

"Had your daddy's back for eighteen years." She teared up. "Would consider it an honor to have yours for eighteen more."

He felt the noose slip around his neck. "Good to know."

She yanked a tissue from the crocheted box cover and dabbed her eyes. "So you're staying?"

The knot at his throat tightened. "If the Board approves an interim position."

"They'd be fools not to."

"I don't know, Shirley. Dad left some pretty big shoes to fill."

"Whether you stay eighteen days or eighteen years, I'll count every minute a blessing. You did a fine job yesterday."

The office phone rang, but Shirley ignored the flashing red light. "Probably just Nola Gay wondering what I've found out about that drifter who passed out in our fellowship hall." Shirley peered over her glasses. "What should I tell her?"

"He's still in the hospital. I don't think he's up for visitors."

"Poor Amy."

"Poor Amy?"

"I'm glad that drifter didn't die on her watch. That girl's suffered more loss than someone her age should ever have to bear."

"What do you mean?"

"Her parents were killed in a car wreck a few years ago."

David's felt his stomach drop. When Amy said she knew how he felt, she was one of the few who'd actually experienced an unexpected tragedy. Even worse, her heartache was double his. He couldn't come close to wrapping his head around such a tragic loss. Now he really felt like a jerk. "I didn't know."

Shirley scurried back around to her seat. Her hand hovered over the ringing phone. "Bette Bob's always been like a second mother to her. That's why Amy came here after she finished nursing school. And let me tell you, if she ever gets her voice back, this town will be doubly blessed. That girl used to sing like an angel."

"What happened to her voice?"

Shirley spun her finger by her ear. "I think it's emotional. 'Course Bette Bob's sayin' it's strained vocal cords or some kind of yet-to-be diagnosed chronic throat infection, but,"— Shirley leaned forward and lowered her voice—"I've read about kids losing their ability to speak after a tragedy and well … I just wish Amy could have sung something for us yesterday. You'd have melted in your pew."

Much as he hated to admit that he'd already experienced Amy's ability to stir all kinds of emotion in him, he was hopeful the little truce they'd negotiated outside the vagrant's hospital room had negated his constant need to smooth things over with her. Whether or not the girl could sing didn't matter to him. Years as a PK had trained his heart to remain solidly in place.

He pointed at the blinking light on Shirley's desk. "Want me to get that phone before Nola Gay has a stroke?"

"Oh, no." Shirley held him off with a flattened palm. "I'm the secretary. You're the pastor."

"Interim."

"We'll see." Shirley picked up the receiver and pressed the light. "Mt. Hope Community Church. How may I serve you?"

David left Shirley to believe what she wanted to believe. Truth was, finding out about Amy's loss had put his commitment issues in perspective. He'd been so wrapped up in his own grief he'd never considered the possibility someone else could hurt worse. His father had always said whenever folks were throwing rocks at the pastor you could almost bet they were hurling their own hurts. Although Amy didn't strike him as someone desperate to have others notice her pain, her experience did explain her lack of patience for his bad humor.

He walked down the dark hall, suddenly very aware that filling in for his father would require more than learning how to prepare a convicting sermon. He had been gone from Mt. Hope for several years. He couldn't assume he still knew everything about everyone in this town. Perhaps it would serve him well to start by taking a fresh look into the lives of the members of Mt. Hope Community Church. Life had changed him. Maybe some of them had also experienced life-changing events.

At his father's door, David shone his phone light on the lock. He turned the key, took another deep breath, and stepped inside.

The scent of books, paper, and his father's cheap aftershave rushed him hard. He flipped on the light. Florescent tubes buzzed and flickered into a blinding glare. Everything was exactly as it had been the day the funeral director brought the Harper family to wait in this room before the funeral service. The private sanctuary hadn't seemed so quiet with Aunt Roxie, Momma, and his sister in the room.

Over Momma's protests, Maxine Davis had furnished the pastor's office with the olive green velvet couch and matching loveseat she'd discarded after a remodel to her husband's Cadillac dealership. That was fifteen years ago. To prove she wasn't completely heartless, Maxine had thrown Momma a bone and let her refinish the bookcases left over from a church garage sale. The shelves sagged with the books and commentaries his father had collected.

David dragged his finger over the book spines as he went to his father's desk. He set his computer bag beside an ancient computer keyboard. This finger-smudged machine was so slow and his father's research books so old, he'd have to use his iPad to score anything current.

A light tap on the door frame startled him. "Nellie?"

Cornelia Davis smiled and flipped her auburn hair over her shoulder. "A guy could get used to pastor's hours, right?"

Shirley barreled past Nellie. "I told her to make an appointment." The secretary planted her stocky body between him and the elder's daughter. "Reverend Harper hasn't even had time to take his coat off, Nellie."

"It's Cornelia, and I didn't know David had been ordained." Nellie took the woman by the shoulder. "The new Reverend's personal life is personal." Nellie moved Shirley aside and marched straight at David. "You did say we needed to catch up, didn't you, David?"

He backed into the desk. "I think that's what *you* said."

Nellie threaded her arm through his and tugged him up against her leopard coat. "Let's get a cup of coffee. I'll buy."

Visions of a dark baptistry room flashed in his mind. David extricated his arm. "Shirley's right." He hurried around the desk. "I've got a lot to do, and I'm not sure where to even start."

Nellie unbuttoned her coat. "That's why I'm here." She let the coat fall seductively from her shoulders to reveal a very tight and flattering low-cut, cream sweater. "You need my help."

Shirley tugged Nellie's coat back up her arm. "I'm here if the Reverend needs help."

David pulled out his father's desk chair. "I've got this, Shirley."

Shirley peered over her glasses. "I'm leaving the door open." She stopped and tugged Nellie's coat over her shoulder one more time before she stomped from the room.

"Put hiring a new secretary on the top of your must-be-done-right-away list." Nellie issued her advice loud enough to make her point for anyone lurking in the hall.

"You didn't get all dolled up just to torment Shirley."

"Glad you noticed." Nellie smiled and let her coat drop to the floor. "I got dolled up to show *you* how serious I am about helping you get what you want."

"And what is that?"

"Board approval."

"I haven't even had time to set up a meeting with them yet."

"Christmas is only a few weeks away." She placed her hands on the desk and leaned forward. The view was equally impressive and discomforting. "You probably haven't started on the Christmas Eve program either."

"It's just barely December." Suddenly very warm, David shrugged out of his jacket and draped it over his father's chair. "Momma's planned the Christmas program for years." He pulled out the chair and sat down. "She's probably already started."

"I've asked around and she's only asked Ivan to play Joseph."

"I'll make a note to see where she's at on the planning."

"Let's talk about your mother's well-being, David." Nellie rolled his name off her tongue like it was a decedent dessert. "Do you really think she's up to it?"

Good question. "The more things can stay the same, the

better. Besides, I think she'll welcome the distraction."

"The Board will be disappointed if Leona just throws something together."

"Momma never just throws something together. But if that's what she has to do this year, the Board will have to get over it."

"Don't be so sure. The Episcopalians are planning a full-fledged candlelight service, complete with wise men and live camels." Her eyes had taken on the cat-like twinkle that always preceded her claws. "Why don't you let me make you *and* your mother look good?" Nellie's painted nails clicked across the desk as she finger-walked her hand toward him.

Pressing himself deep into his father's chair, David said, "I don't know exactly what you're offering."

"You know I've done theater."

"In high school."

She shrugged off his sarcasm and sat down. "Who better to put together a little show?"

"Look, Nellie, I appreciate the offer but I can't impose on your time. Everyone will understand if we limp by this year. Momma can have Wilma play some Christmas carols, I'll read the Christmas story, and maybe Parker can ask Amy Maxwell to sing Silent Night. Shirley tells me she has a great voice…or used to. I think it would encourage her to find it again."

Nellie bristled. "Amy?"

"Bette Bob's niece."

"I know who *Amy* is, David. She used to go to camp with us."

"Are we talking about the same Amy Maxwell?"

Nellie let out a pleased little laugh. "You don't remember the shy, sickly little girl who always had her nose in a medical book?"

"That was Amy?"

"That was me."

David looked up to see Amy standing in the door. Her blonde hair was pulled into a messy bun on the top of her head and her scrubs were wrinkled and stained from a night of work.

"Amy?" In the process of hurriedly pushing his chair back, David nearly flipped over. Arms flailing, he managed to grab the desk and right himself. "We were just talking about you."

"Shirley told me your door was open. She didn't tell me you already had a visitor." Amy tugged at her hospital lanyard. "I should have made an appointment."

"Wait." David motioned for her to come in. "Nellie was telling me that you used to go to camp with us."

Amy shrugged like she didn't know why he was bringing up old news. "Yeah."

He came around the desk. "I'm sorry I didn't recognize you."

"We weren't exactly friends back then. You were three years older and ten times cooler."

"The preacher's son *has* always been a hunk,"—Nellie stood and threaded her arm through his again— "hasn't he?" She raised her hand to her mouth and coughed.

Amy looked from him to Nellie, to the coat on the floor, and back to him. "We can talk later."

"Wait, Amy." David shrugged free of Nellie. "I do remember you. You were the girl who iced my ankle that summer I slid into home base and collided with the catcher." He liked making her eyes sparkle. The permafrost between him and details frozen in time began to melt. "I was so afraid the camp counselors were going to call my parents to come get me, but you had me back in the game in no time."

"It was just a twist."

"And I'm an ingrate."

Nellie butted in. "I brought you a cold drink, David." She coughed again. "Don't you remember?"

The memory of Nellie's hand climbing from his knee to his thigh as he tried to get back out on the playing field sprang from the grave, dragging forth a string of buried memories from that day. Amy had seen the terror in his eyes and cleared her throat, reminding Nellie she was being watched. Nellie had stormed out of the nurse's station in a huff. No telling what Nellie might have tried if the smart girl with glasses hadn't come to his rescue.

"It was a long time ago," David stuttered.

"Nellie, have you checked on that cough?" Amy asked.

"I'm fine," she said, clearing her throat.

"You sound a little hoarse."

"It's just allergies," Nellie insisted.

"Okay." Amy looked at David. "I better go."

"Wait." Once again he found himself chasing after her. This time, he wouldn't let her to get away without making amends. "You've done so much for me, is there something I can do for you?"

"It can wait."

"Nellie was just leaving, weren't you, Nellie?"

Amy cleared her throat in that careful little warning way he remembered from camp. David didn't know if she'd done it on accident or if she, too, remembered the power of that gesture to save him.

One brow lifted over Nellie's calculating stare. "I do have to get on our little project." She picked up her coat and slowly slid her arms through the sleeves. "David's asked me to put together the Christmas show this year. Give his mother a break."

"Momma may not want a—"

"Don't you fret, Handsome. I've got the Harpers' best interest at heart." She flipped her hair out from under her collar. "We'll get that cup of coffee later and I'll give you the rundown on my plans." She kissed David's cheek then shot Amy a triumphant smile. "Good to see you again, Amy."

Before David could make it clear to Nellie that he was never having coffee with her, she was out the door. He was so relieved to see her go he wasn't about to chase after her. He might not have a choice when it came to letting Nellie take over planning the Christmas Eve service, but he could ask Amy to sing himself.

"Come in." He led Amy to the chair still steaming from where Nellie had parked her hot body.

Amy remained standing. "Aunt Bette Bob told me your mother always directed the Christmas Eve program."

"She has for eighteen years."

"Does she know Nellie is taking over?"

He shook his head. "You want to tell her?"

"Thanks, but no."

"It's hard to know how much to keep the same and how much to let change take its natural course."

"Your mother's suffered a shock, but from what my aunt

tells me, she's one tough gal."

He chuckled at the way she'd nailed his mother. "Look, I know it seems like we're always apologizing but I can't let it go that I owe you one. A big one."

"You don't owe me an apology."

"I do."

"David, your twisted ankle happened years ago."

"I'm not talking about icing my ankle. I'm not even talking about not recognizing you, although you have changed."

She smiled. "For the better I hope?"

"I wouldn't say that."

"Thanks."

"No…I mean…I watched you wrap my ankle and I thought you were very pretty then and I think you're even more beautiful now. I'm sorry I was a jerk."

Amy's cheeks flushed. "Because you ignored me at camp?"

"Then, and since then." He pulled the chair up to the desk and indicated she should sit. "I … well … people, in their efforts to offer comfort to my family, have offered all sorts of idiotic platitudes."

Understanding shaped her lips into a perfect O. "And so when I said I know how you feel, you thought I was adding to the useless pile."

Her gentle validation was as soothing as ice on a sprain. "Yeah." He sat on the edge of his father's desk. "Shirley told me about your parents. I'm so sorry." He swallowed the lump in his throat. "Losing Dad was bad. I don't know what I'd do if I'd lost Momma too."

"You'd go on," she said softly. "Maybe not as gallantly as you're trying to go on now, but you'd manage."

Drawn by the incredibly tempting compassion filling her eyes, he leaned forward. "I'd like to hear your story, I mean if you can talk about it."

She sat back, rather surprised. "You'll find out very few people really want to hear about your grief, so your offer is very appealing." She shifted forward, in body and intensity. "But I'm on a short break and the favor I need is more important."

He didn't know why he thought she'd spill her guts to a guy who didn't even remember that she'd once wrapped his ankle. "Sure." He'd racked up quite a bit of debt with this woman and he was anxious to pay some of it off. "Name it."

"I'm not good at asking for help, but I've been thinking…"

He recognized the old drop-a-line-and-wait bait she'd tossed out. Instead of biting, he asked, "Is thinking something new for you?"

If she appreciated his weak attempt at humor, she didn't

allow it to show on her face. "Angus needs more than I can do."

"Doctors having trouble regulating his sugar?"

She shook her head. "His needs are more complicated than managing his diabetes."

"Not sure I'm following."

"Angus needs a chance to get back on his feet. He deserves a second chance at life and ... I was thinking who better to help him go for it than ... the church?"

"You want the church to do what exactly?"

"Rehab him."

"Rehab him?"

"Help him get off the streets and become a productive citizen."

David fell back in his chair. "Are you asking the church to do this, or are you asking me?"

"Well ... aren't they the same?"

"Technically, all of us are the church."

"I know, but you're our leader." Her eyes measured him, not with the same unfriendly appraising sense he'd felt when he'd cornered her in the church sanctuary, but measured, nonetheless.

And, as then, he couldn't explain why he didn't want to seem lacking in her sight. "Look, I'm not even officially the interim pastor yet. Besides, I thought we'd established I'm pretty much winging it."

"You're all we've got." A plea laced her words.

He redirected his gaze to his computer bag and gave letting her down easy his best shot. "I suspect Angus needs family counseling at the very least. This church doesn't have the staff for that."

"The county offers counseling." This woman had an answer for everything. "What this kid needs is a place to stay, one hot meal a day, a job, and a bit of hope."

"Kid?"

She nodded. "He's only sixteen. No parents. He's officially been on his own for six months, but I suspect he was taking care of himself long before his mother died." She leaned in. Her hospital badge scraped across his father's desk. "Angus Freestone needs Jesus."

He drummed his fingers on the desk. Amy had cared for his ankle with the same passion she now infused in this preposterous proposal. To say he wasn't moved once again by her selflessness would be lying. "There might be enough money in the benevolence fund to cover a few nights at the Double D and a couple of blue plate specials at Ruthie's."

She shook her head. "He needs more than a motel room and a hamburger." She reached across the desk and stayed his hand. "He needs role models. People who care about him." Her touch was a fire that spread up his arm and flushed his cheeks. "I know how important it was for me when Aunt Bette Bob took me under her wing."

David slowly released a trapped sigh. "Maddie will be out of town until Christmas Eve doing residency interviews. I guess Angus could stay in her room."

"No, I wasn't asking your family to take him," Amy argued. "Your mother's got enough to deal with since your grandmother got kicked out of rehab. Poor Leona hasn't had one quiet minute to process her grief. I'm not asking her to take on another houseguest, especially one we don't know much about."

"A couple of weeks ago, Momma could have taken the guy in with one hand tied behind her back, and she would have, but now—"

"Mt. Hope is full of good people, David."

The way she said his name, he could almost believe she thought he was one of them. "I guess the least I can do as interim pastor is help you find someone."

She smiled, her first true smile since he'd met her. A smile that lit her eyes with an angelic glow. A smile that made him wish he could give her the moon.

CHAPTER SIX

David paced the slick sidewalk in front of Dewey Hardware. He blew into his cupped hands while watching for Momma's van. He'd practiced all sorts of different arguments for the decision he'd made on his walk from the church and none of them would hold up in Momma's courtroom.

"Hey, David." Ruthie waved to him from the partially open door of the Koffee Kup café next door. "How about a cup of coffee while you wait?"

"Thanks, but Momma should be here any minute."

Ruthie stepped outside, rubbing her hands over her crossed arms. "Saul's in here polishing off a burger. He won't be in the mood to tackle your father's estate until he finishes his second cup of coffee."

Obviously attorney-client privilege didn't count for much in

Mt. Hope. Saul had probably passed his father's will around the diner and everyone had already formed their laments for the destitute widow.

He'd love to give this small-town lawyer a piece of his mind, but it might be wiser to pump the guy for info. That way he could have a mental list of options prepared for his devastated mother. "Can you fry me a burger too, Ruthie?"

Her grin exposed the gap between her front teeth. "One double cheese, everything but onions coming up."

David sent his mother a quick text asking her to meet him at the diner before their meeting with Saul.

Smells of fried meat, coffee, and pancake syrup stirred forgotten memories of the Saturday fishing trips David used to take with his dad. Long before the sun rose, he and his dad would climb into the van which they'd stocked the night before with fishing poles and a cooler of iced soft drinks. On their way to their favorite pond, they'd stop by the Koffee Kup for what his father called fortification for the fun ahead. Hamburgers for breakfast had been their little secret…something they'd never told Momma. What else had his father kept from Momma?

David spotted Saul Levy in the back booth. The trim man with a military buzz cut and a tidy push-broom moustache sat facing the door and reading the paper. David strode past the long counter with its display of meringue pies under glass domes and a chalk board with Today's Specials written in Ruthie's shaky hand. He wove through the eclectic mix of people filling the tables. A few truckers had parked their rigs two blocks away and braved the cutting wind for a saucer-sized slice of Ruthie's pies. A big-bellied cop shoveled a tall stack of pancakes into his mouth. His holstered gun seemed like overkill in this small town. The usual coffee klatch of old men had shoved two tables together so they could regurgitate the news and argue over the price of everything.

David stopped at Saul's table and pulled himself to his full height. "Mr. Levy?" David extended his hand. "David Harper."

Saul lowered his paper and promptly checked his watch. "Wasn't expecting you for another ten minutes."

David let his unshaken hand slide inside his pocket. "I'm early."

"I see that." Lawyer Levy did not extend an invitation for David to sit.

David boldly dropped into the booth anyway. "I was hoping you could give me a little advance information on what Momma might expect."

A slight twitch tugged at Saul's poker-face expression. "I don't know what kind of lawyer you are, but this one never breaks lawyer-client privilege, even for members of the client's family."

Bristling at the reprimand, along with the fact that he'd obviously been wrong about this tight-lipped attorney, David slid to the edge of the seat then stopped. "How did you know I was a lawyer?"

"Your father was very proud of you."

The unexpected praise was another stone on David's growing stack of guilt.

"Double cheese." Ruthie plopped David's favorites on the table. "No onions and I threw in those curly fries you used to order for breakfast with your daddy." She wiped her hands on her apron. "This one's on me."

"Thanks, Ruthie but—"

She raised a palm cracked from years in dishwater. "I could never repay your daddy for all the business he sent my way." Ruthie swiped the back of her hand across her brow. "Don't let them fries go cold." She left David staring at the steaming burger tucked inside a golden, grilled bun.

Saul laid his knife and fork neatly across the top of his spotless plate and cocked his head. "You heard the woman. Eat up."

"I'll just move on and let you finish your lunch in peace."

"Don't be stupid, boy. If I wanted to chew you up and spit you out, you wouldn't still be upright."

"Good to know." Having been made to feel like a naughty boy, David busied himself with the ketchup. He squirted a glob near his fries, dipped the tip of one of the curls in sauce, then crammed it into his mouth. Salty goodness exploded on his tongue as powerful eyes drilled him from across the table. Two-handing his burger, David looked over the bun and dared to meet the scrutiny coming at him from a man he didn't even know.

Saul held up his empty coffee cup. After the diner owner waddled over, he said, "Ruthie, you need to hire more help."

"When I get some better tippers, maybe I can afford help." She topped Saul off and picked up his empty plate. "Might even take a little vacation." She nodded at David. "Need anything?"

"I'm good," he said around the mouthful of delicious beef. "Thanks, Ruthie."

"Stick around and I'll put some meat on those bones." With an exhausted sigh, Ruthie waddled back to the counter.

The beady-eyed lawyer thumped a packet of sugar. "According to the local gossip, you never practiced and don't plan to. That true?"

"Like you said, word gets around." Grease running down his chin, David chewed on why the sober man stirring a sugar into his coffee would care. "Sometimes you just have to wait and see what turns up fact or fiction."

Saul tapped his spoon on the rim of the cup. "You know, your mother is stronger than you think, right?"

David wasn't sure what galled him more: Saul's negative opinion of David's unwillingness to take up the vocation for which he'd trained or the man's favorable opinion of his mother. He choked down his bite and opened his mouth to respond.

"Sorry I got tied up." Momma stood over them. The wind had blown her hair and she wobbled on those red heels she'd worn to church the way she did when her feet were killing her, but her usual can-do smile was perfectly in place. "Saul."

Saul wiped his moustache, scooted out from his seat, and stood. "Leona." A crisp wave of his hand offered her his place. "May I buy you a cup of coffee?"

Momma shook her head. "I hate to rush our meeting, but Ivan wants me to cover the school board meeting tonight. Modyne's not feeling well."

"No problem." Saul motioned for the check. "Add David's to mine," he told Ruthie.

"We're not a charity case." David slid out from the bench, stood, and sandwiched his mother between him and Saul. He pulled a twenty from his wallet and put it on top of the check in Ruthie's outstretched hand. "Keep the change, Ruthie."

Momma gave him the look that said they'd talk about his rude behavior later, then she followed the attorney to his office.

Saul Levy's office was as sharp and put together as he was. Photos of him wearing his crisp Air Force uniform and shaking hands with senators and two different presidents lined his walls. He led them to a conference room with windows that overlooked Main Street. A gleaming walnut table with eight leather chairs took up most of the large space. At one end of the table, a thin file folder waited.

"Have a seat, Leona." Saul pulled out a chair for Momma. Once she was settled, he claimed the place at the head of the table and motioned for David to join them opposite Momma. Eyes sharply assessing their moods, Saul put his elbows on the table, clasped his hands above the file, and waited for their full attention. "Are you expecting your daughter, Leona?"

"Maddie's unavailable." David intended for his abrupt insertion to draw the line on how this meeting was going to go. He was pleased the move had raised Saul's brow.

"Very well." Saul laid a palm on the file. "Shall we begin?"

Momma's knuckles were white on the handles of the purse in her lap as she stared at the file. "I didn't even know J.D. had written a will."

"Although your husband was a very public man, he held

his privacy in high regard. Unlike most folks in this town, I believe a pastor should have that right." Saul tapped the file. "The will is standard." He reached inside and retrieved two thin documents. He passed one to Momma and one to David. "I have a copy I can send to Maddie if you'll tell me where to send it."

"I'll see that she gets her copy." David held out his hand, withholding the information that Maddie had popped in early to surprise Momma before she had to fly around the country for residency interviews. "She'll be home for Christmas."

"Have her drop in for her copy." Saul's version of drawing his own lines. "While the will is straightforward, there is the issue of distributing the assets."

"Assets?" Momma's voice was shaky. "What assets?"

"There aren't many." Saul pulled out another piece of paper. "A life insurance policy."

"Life insurance?" Momma's eyes widened. "Really?"

"It's only twenty thousand." Saul slid the paper to Momma. "I'm afraid that won't go far."

"No," Momma agreed. "Almost half will go to the funeral home."

Saul nodded in restrained commiseration. "There's no savings account."

"It's always been hard to save when"— Momma

swallowed—"there's barely been enough money for the checking account."

David cringed at the injustice of Momma having her personal finances laid bare. "Do we really have to drag her through—"

"J.D. did, however"—Saul continued, his steely eyes cutting from David and back to Momma—"own several stocks in a little known Singapore-based pharmaceutical corporation. TauRx. They're presently researching Alzheimer's disease. No one knows the value of this asset."

"Stock? We couldn't afford stock," Momma said.

David couldn't contain his shock. "Why would Dad invest in Asian pharmaceuticals?"

"His mother," Momma answered stoically. "She died after a long, slow descent into dementia. J.D. was terrified the same would happen to him." She opened her bag and removed a tissue. "I guess it was God's grace that J.D. died so suddenly and with his mind still so sharp."

Saul's hand covered Momma's. "We won't know what impact these stocks will have on your future until we marshal the assets."

Momma's face puzzled. "Marshal the assets?" She removed her hand and David was glad.

He didn't like the way this lawyer looked at his mother. The guy wasn't wearing a wedding ring. If he thought his freedom entitled him to prey on this grieving widow, he had another thing coming. "Saul means Dad's little investment could end up costing us a bucket-load of taxes."

"Taxes?" Her eyes grew wide. "I can barely pay this month's light bill. How am I going to pay the IRS?" Momma glanced at David's face and immediately retracted her fear. "This is not your worry, David. It's mine."

"Let's not jump to conclusions," Saul interjected. "Let me find out if the shares J.D. owned even meet the taxable thresholds."

"But the income still has to be reported, right?" David clarified.

"Yes."

Momma exhaled slowly. "Guess I better not pay off any other bills until we know how much I owe the IRS." She closed her purse, pushed her chair back, and offered Saul her hand. "Thank you, Mr. Levy."

"Saul, please." The lawyer rose to his feet. "I'm here if you need me, Leona."

David took his mother by the elbow. "We'll let you know, *Mister* Levy."

CHAPTER SEVEN

Three days later, Amy guided Angus from the edge of the bed to the waiting wheelchair.

"I can walk," her wobbly patient insisted.

She hoped his growing independence was an indication of his improved health rather than a sign that she'd made a big mistake. Either way, the system couldn't keep him any longer. "Hospital policy."

He dropped into the seat. "I'm not a baby."

She straightened and faced him. "Starting today you'll have plenty of opportunity to prove it." She hung his filthy backpack over the handles, grateful she'd convinced him to let her launder his clothes last night. "The church is giving you the chance at a life that living on the streets never will."

"Why are you doing this?"

"I believe you're the type of guy who doesn't make the same mistake twice." It had felt good when David recognized she was smart and determined. She hoped Angus would eventually begin to believe the same about himself. "And the members of Mt. Hope Community Church believe everyone deserves a second chance."

Angus started to get up. "Not sticking around so some lame pastor can preach at me all day."

"I can promise you, I won't preach." David stood in the door, his hair mussed and his cheeks red from the cold wind. "Ready?"

"Who are you?" Angus asked.

Amy flashed David teasing look. "He's Mt. Hope's lame pastor."

"You don't look like no preacher I've ever seen."

David crossed his arms and leaned against the door frame. "Well, I'm all you've got. Take it or leave it."

Angus looked from David to Amy. "My mom used to say folks in Texas were bossy. It's why she lit out first chance she got."

"Your mother from Texas, was she?" Amy asked.

Angus shrugged. "Maybe."

"A storm's rolling in." David nodded toward the gray skies outside the window. "There's a place at my house where you can have a warm bed and full belly to ride it out, or you can sleep under the overpass. Choice is yours, Angus."

"Your house?" Amy asked David, confused by the change in his plan to find someone else.

"Yep." Something in the way David avoided looking directly at her told her he wasn't telling her everything. "Momma's hospitality is legendary."

Once they had Angus settled, the least she could do would be to grab a private moment and propose a schedule to lighten the Harpers' load. "Give this a chance, Angus. Please."

The boy looked from her to David. "Guess I don't got much of a choice."

"Everyone's got a choice," David told Angus. "What we make of them is always up to us."

Angus waved his finger between David and Amy. "You two married or something?" Angus plopped back into the chair. "You sure sound alike."

David cut his eyes her way and smiled. "Just good friends, on the same page."

Amy hoped David hadn't noticed the flush his assessment of their relationship had brought to her face. "I think we've got everything."

*****

Moving Angus into Maddie's room consisted of hanging

the boy's thin hoodie on a door knob and showing him where to store his hospital toothbrush and toothpaste.

"I've never seen so much pink." Angus fingered one of the ruffled curtains. "Your sister really win all these trophies?"

"She's an overachiever." David clapped Angus on the shoulder. "Tomorrow we'll see about finding you some more clothes. In the meantime, a few house rules."

"Knew this gig was too good to be true." Angus fell back on the bed and slung his feet up on the ruffled bedspread.

"Rule number one. No shoes on the bed." David tapped Angus on the foot and waited until the boy complied. "Dinner is always at six. There's only one TV in the house. You're welcome to turn it on for the six o'clock news, but Momma turns it off at nine. No drugs, alcohol, or smoking. Ever. And you will be expected to attend church."

"Juvie has less rules."

"Sooner or later everyone has to play by the rules." David closed the guestroom door and took Amy by the elbow. "Juvie? That's a little unnerving."

"Guess I should have investigated more than his medical history. I didn't—"

David stopped and took her by the shoulders. "Hey, this isn't all on you. I agreed to this evil plan."

"Evil?"

"Okay, far reaching." His eyes had become a well of strength she could easily fall into. "We'll give this hands-and-feet-of-Jesus thing our best shot. Things don't work out, we'll see what kind of state or county help is out there for him, okay?"

Amy nodded, reassured by his confidence. "Okay."

"But I'm still going to sleep with one eye open." Whenever David teased her it was as if the weight of the world left his shoulders, and she suspected this preacher's son had carried heavy burdens long before he decided to take his father's place. "Come on." David's hand touched the small of her back. "Angus could probably use a moment to get used to all the pink, and I could use some help deciphering the boy's med schedule."

"What will we do with Angus when Maddie gets home?"

"I guess it'll give us an excuse to get together and work it out."

"Guess so." Amy followed David to the parsonage kitchen, her tummy quivering at the easy way he'd said get together.

Tater scurried from his bed by the back door. David knelt and gave the dog a good scratch behind the ears. "I'll let him out and then make us some coffee."

She'd been in this stately old house several times, mostly for wedding showers or ladies teas with her aunt. As she watched David play with the dog, fill the Keurig, and search for clean cups in the dishwasher, the parsonage took on an unexpected hominess. The kind of home she'd always dreamed of. Amy crossed her arms over her chest and rubbed at the emptiness running through her veins.

"You cold?" David set two cups on the counter. "I can turn up the heat, but you'll be frozen stiff before our ancient system kicks in." He took off his jacket. As he wrapped the heavy leather around her shoulders, she melted into the warmth of having him so close. For a moment they stood toe to toe, David's hands clutching the jacket collar. Breathing the same air, neither speaking, their eyes locked. He was going to kiss her and even though she knew better than to let her defenses down, she wanted to taste his hard-won smile.

Tater scratched at the door.

"Better let him in," Amy whispered. "Before he claws his way in."

David's hands dropped from the collar of his jacket. "Yeah." He wheeled and went to the kitchen door. Tater shot in and went straight to her.

She bent and rubbed his soft head. "You've got a dog clawing to get in and a boy clawing to get out."

"Tater's a pretty astute judge of character. He knows a good thing when he sees it. Hopefully, Angus will too." David opened a cabinet. "Momma keeps a stash of flavored coffees squirreled away somewhere. That'll get your blood pumping."

Her blood was already thrumming. A hot drink was the last thing she needed. "You don't have to wait on me."

"I owe you a cup, remember? Besides, I make a mean cup of coffee and I'm hoping it'll make up for my poor start on this friendship thing I bragged about to Angus."

"Nursing our friendship to that level is going to require a hamburger at a minimum."

His grin activated those dimples she'd noticed before. "Ruthie's. Tomorrow at noon?"

"Agreed." Amy pulled out a chair at the kitchen table. Why had she let those dark brown eyes entice her into thinking she could have what she'd always wanted. She'd encouraged him. She shouldn't have and it would stop here and now. If she didn't stop playing with fire she would get burned and worse yet, David would get hurt. She couldn't bear the thought of adding to his pain.

It was time to change the subject and fast. Tomorrow, she'd deal with how to shut her feelings down and keep their relationship where it had to remain: two friends focused on the mutual success of rehabbing one very scared, sick kid. "So why is Angus staying here?"

"I wanted to keep an eye on him."

"You couldn't find anyone else?"

His gaze seemed to go straight to her heart. "Didn't ask."

She could see his decision was wrapped up in some sort of desire to please her, and yet she had to ask, "Why not?"

He gave an uncomfortable little shrug and returned to rummaging through the cabinets. "Dad wouldn't have asked anyone to do anything he wasn't willing to do himself."

"I see." Why was she disappointed? She didn't want their relationship to be anything more than a joint social project. "So what did your mom say when you sprung this plan on her?"

"Uh..." David stopped his rummaging around in the cabinets. "I didn't exactly get a chance to talk to her about it."

"Leona doesn't know?"

David closed his eyes and shook his head.

"Your mother is going to come home from a very long day on the job and discover she's got a boarder...a juvenile delinquent boarder?"

"I told you I'm not good at this pastor thing yet."

"This is more of a *son* thing, don't you think?"

He leaned against the counter. "Momma started Dad's probate stuff today. It was a lot to take in."

Sinking realization dawned on Amy. "And so final."

David crossed to her and pulled out the chair next to her.

He spun it around and straddled the seat and let the back support his crossed arms. He was so close his uneven breaths punctuated the struggle in his mind. "After your parents died, did you discover they had … secrets?"

"Secrets?"

"You know, things that surprised you? Things they might have done? Things that totally changed your perception of them?" His eyes were dark wells begging her to jump. His loaded questions would require personal revelations she should sidestep if she wanted them to remain no more than friends.

She shifted in her seat. "Actually, I did." She hadn't told anyone what she was about to tell him. "When I was cleaning out my mother's closet, I found a drawer filled with sexy lingerie."

His brows peaked. "Yeah?"

"And a stack of love letters from my father." For some reason, she wasn't embarrassed to tell him everything that had gone through her mind as she packed away the silky garments. "I knew my parents loved each other. It was obvious to anyone who met them. But, it had never occurred to me that they'd had a healthy, active, possibly even very sensual sex life."

"That bothered you?"

"At first, and then it explained everything. It explained how they could be in a room full of people and it was like everyone else just disappeared. Even me sometimes. Crazy thing is, their passionate love for each other made me feel very secure."

"Crazy, right?"

She poked his arm. "Does that mean your parents embarrassed you, too?"

"I can tell you've never been a PK."

"PK?"

"Preacher's kid." He dragged his hand over the stubble on his face. "Momma lit up like a rock star groupie every time Dad took the pulpit. After church they had this way of finding each other in the crowd, their hands lightly brushing, their eyes only on each other. Maddie and I used to call it their private room." He made air quotes around the word private. "But their intense commitment to each other…filled this house, filled the church, and made a difference in this town." David gripped the back of the chair. "I know people move on. They have to. In a few months, most people will hardly remember the Reverend J.D. Harper." David's knuckles whitened and his eyes rose to hers. "For Momma's sake, I can't let that happen."

This peek behind the curtain David kept drawn over the

window of his heart brought with it a surprisingly powerful desire to see him succeed. Amy laid her hand over his. "Is that why you agreed to rehab Angus Freestone?"

"That and"—his gaze was an intoxicating gleam of challenge—"because maybe someday I want someone to look at me the way my mother looked at my father."

CHAPTER EIGHT

Leona closed the oven door and dried her hands. It felt good to be cooking for a small army and to have the house buzzing with activity. The only thing missing was J.D.'s booming voice at the card game David had insisted Angus join in the dining room. If J.D. were here, her life would feel almost normal.

Leona went to the boom box on the counter and pushed play on her *Gaither Christmas Favorites* CD. As the music poured over her, she imagined J.D.'s arms sweeping her around the kitchen. They'd never had a formal dance lesson. They'd always been so in sync, they hadn't needed them, or so she thought.

J.D. had invested money they didn't have in some crazy stock, and it had never crossed her mind he had a secret.

"That new stray you took in is a card shark." The

unexpected voice of her mother caused Leona to jump with a start.

She turned to find her mother decked out in a lovely sweater set and matching slacks and sitting primly in her wheelchair. "Mother, I didn't hear you."

"You always did love Christmas music."

"J.D. gave me that CD."

"He was generous to a fault, unlike me." Roberta wheeled her chair into the kitchen. "I lost nearly two dollars to that new kid."

Leona picked up the chopping board and scraped onions into the hot skillet. "Maybe you've met your match, Mother."

"Or maybe you need to lock up the silver...oh, wait...you don't have any."

"Waiting to inherit yours."

"Don't hold your breath. I've no intention of giving up any time soon."

Leona chuckled at the comfort level growing between her and her mother. Before her mother's accidental fall down the stairs, they could scarcely speak a civil word to each other. Now, here they were teasing. Who would have thought a deeper relationship with her prickly mother would've been a byproduct of the fight that had ended in Roberta's broken hip? Proof God could take something awful and shape it into something good, J.D. would have said. Maybe the same would come from his deception.

"On second thought,"—Roberta's tone was thoughtful—"you can have it now."

"What would I do with real silver?" Leona waved her paring knife over her mother's outfit. "Real silver belongs with the woman who still dresses for dinner."

Roberta brushed imaginary lint from her cashmere pants. "I didn't send Melvin all the way back to the city to fetch this outfit from my closet so I could eat sloppy joes with your growing menagerie." Mother pushed at the back of her freshly coiffed hair, a habit she'd used to intimidate others for years. "I have dinner plans."

"Plans?" Leona rinsed a couple of tomatoes. "Are you sure you're feeling up to plans?"

"It's just dinner out."

"Dinner out?" Leona turned off the faucet. "In this *godforsaken town,* as you so lovingly call Mt. Hope?"

"There's a new Mexican restaurant on Main."

"Ivan asked me to cover their grand opening next week." Leona set the tomatoes on the counter and wiped her hands on a towel. "How did you know about it?"

"I was invited to their soft opening, a quiet, little dinner to thank their investors."

"You must have hit your head harder than the doctors thought if you invested in a Mexican restaurant in a dying town."

Roberta tugged at one of her diamond earrings. "I'm a *guest* of an investor."

"Look at you making friends. Next thing you know, you might even start coming to church."

"Don't press your luck, Leona."

"Is Melvin taking you?"

"Not that it is any of your business, but no."

Leona decided not to play her mother's little game of cat and mouse. Even without a hip injury, the woman hadn't driven herself anywhere in years. She probably didn't even possess a valid driver's license anymore. The mystery dinner date would have to show his, or her, face soon enough. All Leona had to do was wait. She returned to her browning meat.

"So how long is that boy staying?" Roberta asked.

"I don't know, but thanks for being such a good sport about having an extra mouth to feed in the house."

"Contrary to popular belief, I had a broken hip, not a defective heart. Anyone in their right mind can see the boy needs help...and I'm not talking about Angus."

Leona took up her spoon, ready to defend her son. "David

will find himself."

"David doesn't know it, but he *has* found himself." Roberta wheeled to the table and started folding napkins. "But that's not what's worrying him."

"David's worrying?"

"Yes." Roberta ran her finger along the crease of fabric. "I'm not judging you, dear, you've had quite a bit on your plate."

"Mother, I don't know what you're trying to say so just spit it out."

"Ever since you and David met with that small town lawyer...what's his name?"

"Saul. Saul Levy."

"Sounds Jewish to me. Which is good."

"What does his ethnicity have to do with anything?"

"If anybody can squeeze a dollar out of a nickel, I should think he'd be your man."

"For your information, Saul has been a Christian for years."

Roberta's shoulders sagged. "So much for that ray of hope."

"Mother, what is going on?"

"David seems determined to save you."

Leona sighed. "I've told him I'm not his problem."

"Well, he's right. Someone has to save you from yourself."

Roberta dropped the napkins and wheeled over to the stove. "I don't think you can trust God to sweep the problems with your future under the rug."

"Mother, trusting God doesn't mean I expect my problems to magically disappear."

"David told me you could possibly owe the IRS a great deal of money."

"I wish he hadn't aired our dirty laundry."

"The boy didn't broadcast your financial straits from the pulpit, Leona. He told his grandmother."

"Who just happens to be very rich."

"Which is why you can't turn down my offer."

"What offer?"

"Let me pay whatever taxes are owed the IRS so that you can use whatever is left of J.D.'s life insurance as a down payment on your future."

Leona was floored. Her first thought was that maybe the doctors had accidentally replaced her mother's heart instead of her hip after her Thanksgiving tumble down the parsonage staircase. Tater's sudden barking drowned out the protests that surfaced next. The dog rushed the man coming through the kitchen door.

"Cotton?" Leona's surprise changed to fear. "Is something wrong at the church?"

The white-haired church janitor's tanned cheeks were red from the cold. "That church building can get along without us for an evening, Leona." When he brushed at the flakes of snow on his sports coat, Leona realized he was dressed in slacks, button-down shirt, and a spiffy new tie. "I'm here to pick up my date."

Leona's mouth dropped open. "Date?"

"He means me," Roberta smiled proudly. "Cotton is the mystery investor you wouldn't dare ask me to divulge."

"I don't know that I would have believed you, Mother."

"If there's one thing I'm tired of being, it's predictable." Roberta's push at the back of her perfectly-teased hair.

"In that case, you're nailing it," Leona said, unable to stop the grin spreading across her face.

Not quite sure what was going on, Cotton turned to Roberta. "Bertie, you're pretty as a picture."

Leona couldn't help but notice the glow on her mother's face. Never in a million years would she have guessed Cotton was the reason her mother had lost her razor-sharp edge and offered financial help without her usual strings and condescension.

The meat on the stove began to burn. Leona lowered the flame and grabbed the wooden spoon. While she shoved the darkened pieces of meat around, Cotton wheeled Roberta out the front door.

Leona shut off the burner and picked up the phone.

Maddie answered on the first ring. "Momma? Everything okay?"

Leona didn't even ask how her interviews where going. She just jumped in with the question that had been burning in her mind since her visit to Saul Levy's office. "Did you know your father had invested in Alzheimer's research?"

"No."

"Well, I guess it just goes to show that you can know someone your whole life and never really know them."

CHAPTER NINE

Over the clink of cutlery, Ruthie shouted lunch orders at the diner's fry cook. David waited in the same booth where he'd met his father's attorney the day before. He didn't think anyone could make him feel more edgy or foolish than the steely-eyed, ex-JAG lawyer. Unfortunately, he'd made that assumption before he spilled his guts to the blonde nurse who'd agreed to meet him for a burger. Why had he opened himself up? Made himself vulnerable to judgment? Hadn't he learned anything growing up in the parsonage?

Telling Amy he'd like to have someone special to love had scared her. She bolted so fast she'd nearly mowed Momma down on her way out the door. But Amy's reaction hadn't shaken him as much as the realization he wanted a committed relationship like the one his parents had and, more unsettling still, he wanted to commit to her.

Which was crazy.

They barely knew one another. And it wasn't like they were a match made in heaven. So far, their common interests consisted of the good of Mt. Hope Community Church and a sick, screwed-up kid named Angus. It would serve him right if Amy stood him up and left him to sort out these troubles on his own.

"My replacement ran late." Amy slid into the seat across from him, her cheeks red from the cold, her sparkling eyes hopeful. "How'd it go with your mom? She agree to Angus staying?"

Relieved Amy had given their unusual relationship another chance, David grinned. "Not much throws Momma off her game."

"Didn't know you could be so persuasive."

"I'm not. Momma said a project might be just what this church needs right now, and she could see how focusing on someone less fortunate would be good for her."

"Does your mother always put others before herself?"

"Pretty much."

"I guess that makes you a combination of both parents."

"How so?"

"Giving up your dreams for the good of someone else."

The admiration in her voice surprised him. "It's pretty crowded on the Harper family pedestal. Don't try to squeeze me in between my parents."

"Taking on a homeless kid won't be easy...for any of us," Amy removed the scarf around her neck. "I don't think I made myself clear, but I plan to help. Meals. Taking Angus to job interviews. Getting the boy enrolled in school."

"Look, Amy, I need to say something before we tackle the Angus situation."

"That sounds ominous. Are you changing your mind, because I can be pretty persuasive?"

Her eyes sparkled with a determination he found irresistible. Better find something else to focus on or he'd be done in again. He toyed with the paper wrapper holding the silverware bundle together. "This is not about Angus." Keep it short and sweet, he told himself. Don't scare her off again. "I shouldn't have made that crack about us...you...my future." Why did his tongue become a loose cannon whenever she was within firing range? When her hair cupped her shoulders and her eyes lacked any of the scorn he deserved, trusting himself to say what needed to be said and then shutting up was harder than it should be.

"Take a chill pill, David." She tossed her scarf on the seat and retrieved the laminated menu card stashed behind the smudged metal napkin holder. "You deserve someone who wants what you want in life. I'm praying you find her." She lowered her eyes and dragged her finger down the limited selection. "Which burger do you get?"

The dropping sensation in his chest wasn't congruent with her quick willingness to let him off the hook. "Don't you want a family someday?"

"This angst you're feeling isn't about me." She returned the menu to the rack, put her elbows on the table, and crossed her arms. "It's about you."

"Why do women always make everything about someone else?"

"Why do men always change the subject when a woman asks them to talk about their feelings?" She wasn't letting him off the hook.

If he wanted things to move forward, he'd have to once again risk letting her see behind the curtain he'd drawn years ago. "Momma's in trouble and she's wasting what little energy she has left worrying about me."

"Grief has its stages. People have to walk through each phase at their own pace and in their own way."

"It's more than grief. Dad didn't..." He smacked his fisted hand against his palm, mentally beating himself up for saying anything. "Never mind."

"You're grieving, too." Amy's hand covered his fist. The jolt passed through his clenched fingers and lit up his body. "After my parents died, the hole they left was so big, I..." she paused. "May I pass on the advice my aunt gave me? Don't do anything drastic—"

"For a year, I know."

"You've already made some pretty major changes. Quit school. Moved to a different continent. Put your career aside to take your father's place. The ground is shifting beneath your shoes. I can vouch for the importance of finding a friend who understands. My aunt's been that friend for me." She squeezed his hand, the one she still held. The general sense of uneasiness she could stir within him kicked into high alert. "I'd like to be that friend for you."

He pulled free. "Friends?" Maybe he was too deep in grief to see things clearly, but he could've sworn he'd seen their relationship going a totally different direction. "A pastor can't have too many *friends*, can he?"

"David, I can't be more—"

"You lovebirds ready?" Ruthie appeared at their booth, her pad and pencil poised to take down their orders. "The fried chicken livers are real good today."

Amy's cheeks flushed. "I'll have the chef salad. Ranch on the side. And sweet tea, please, Ruthie."

"Usual for you, David?" Ruthie asked.

"I think I'll have what my *friend* is having."

Ruthie's brow shot up. "For David to change his order, I'd say y'all are way more than friends." She rubbed her back.

"Just friends." David and Amy blurted simultaneously.

Ruthie's hand moved in circles over her back as she eyed them both. "Two salads it is." She drew her hand around with a pained groan and scribbled on her pad.

"You okay, Ruthie?" Amy asked.

"I went to see that new doc in town." Ruthie stuffed her notepad in her apron pocket. "He took one look at me and said I can't be on my feet twelve hours a day anymore." She waved her hands to indicate the full diner. "But do y'all see that cute little doctor bussing these tables or hauling burgers so I can sit down?"

"Sounds like you need help, Ruthie." Amy's eyes twinkled. "Doesn't she, David?"

David shrugged. "We can get our own tea if that'll help."

"We can do more than fill our own glasses." Amy's eyes pleaded for his support. "Can't we, David?"

"I guess we could clear our table," he mumbled, still stinging.

Amy landed a stealthy kick to his shin.

"Ouch." David's nose was still out of joint from the door

Amy had slammed in his face. He didn't appreciate the blow below the belt. "In case you haven't noticed, I kind of have my charitable hands full at the moment."

"Exactly." Obviously exasperated, Amy took over the conversation. "Ruthie, what you need is some younger blood. Someone who could keep up with the demands of your business and give you that much-needed break."

Comprehension snapped David out of his funk. "You mean Angus?"

"Angus?" Ruthie shook her head in pity. "Who'd name a fella after a cow?"

"Truth is, Ruthie," Amy began to explain. "We don't know a lot about him but the boy is sixteen and—"

"Smart." David added, anxious to steer the conversation back to the one thing he and Amy could agree upon. "You'll have him trained in no time."

"I see what y'all are up to." Ruthie waved her pencil in their faces. "Angus is that vagrant who fell out at your church, right?"

"Yes, but—"

Ruthie held up her palm and put a stop to their less than stellar sales job. "What makes y'all think I'd want some drifter near my cash register?"

"You're right, Ruthie," David said. "It's not right to expect you to help the kid get back on his feet."

"Darn tootin'," Ruthie said. "I ain't runnin' no charity. If word got out that I took in one of those drifters, they'd stack up on my doorstep faster than my cook can say *order up*."

David couldn't stand the disappointment on Amy's face. "His name's Angus Freestone and he isn't asking for handouts—"

"Freestone?" The flush drained from Ruthie's cheeks and she swayed like she might pass out.

"David!" Amy scrambled to the edge of her seat. "She's going down."

Ruthie regained enough composure to signal Amy to scoot over. "Sixteen, you say?" She dropped into the booth and whispered, "I'll take him."

CHAPTER TEN

Walmart sack in hand, David bounded up the stairs with the things he and Amy had purchased for Angus. Their dash through the store had been so much fun David had almost forgotten they would never be more than friends.

"He's sixteen, not sixty. No flannel," Amy had said as she playfully hung the shirt he'd chosen back on the rack. "Angus will look great in this zippered sweatshirt," she'd held up her choice like she'd caught a ten-pound bass.

"I don't think it matters what he wears," he'd argued. "Ruthie acted like she'd take him sight unseen."

"You never get a second chance to make a good first impression."

David smiled at the memory of Amy dropping the jacket in the cart and leaving him to contemplate the bad first impression he'd made on her and the tactic he'd have to employ to obliterate that rule.

David rapped his knuckles on Maddie's bedroom door. "Angus, got something for you."

"It's open."

David walked in, half-expecting to find his sister's room trashed. Instead, the bedspread didn't have a crease or wrinkle, nothing on any of the shelves had been touched, and Angus was sitting cross-legged on the floor with his hands in his lap. "Who taught you how to make a bed, Angus?"

"No one. Why?"

"These crisp corners look like Momma made it."

Angus shrugged.

Something wasn't right. "You haven't slept in it, have you, man?"

"I'm good on the floor."

"When I said no feet on the bed, I didn't mean you couldn't pull the sheet back and sleep there."

"This carpet is way thicker than the ground I've been bunking down on."

"We'll argue about where you catch some shut-eye later." David tossed him the sack. "You need to hit the shower."

"Took one at the hospital."

"That was a few days ago."

"Gone longer."

"Not while you live here, and not before you have your first job interview."

Angus's brow furrowed. "Job interview?"

"Yep. Thirty minutes." David pointed toward the hall. "Hit the shower and shave while you're in there. Everything you need is in the bag."

Angus clambered to his feet. "Uh …" He stood there, shuffling the sack from hand to hand. "Uh …"

"Something wrong?"

"Never shaved before."

"What do you mean you've never shaved?"

"Don't know how," he mumbled.

"Didn't your father—" The embarrassment on Angus' face stopped David cold. "It's not hard. Come on. I'll show you."

David trailed Angus into the bathroom. He opened the bag of disposable razors, laid one on the counter, then shook the shaving cream can. He turned on the faucet. "Once you douse your face with hot water, put the toilet lid down and take a seat."

Angus complied. He sat, his hands braced on his knees, water dripping from the straggly red hairs sprouting from his chin. Wide-eyed he watched David pop the guard from the blade. "This going to hurt?"

"Only if you keep talking and squirming around."

David set the razor aside and filled his palm with creamy lather. He gazed into Angus' terrified brown eyes. "Men shave every day and live to tell about it." David could feel the boy trembling as he spread the lather. "Relax, man. I gotcha."

The day David's own father taught him to shave in this very bathroom sprang to mind. Dad had followed the trail of blood from the bathroom to where David was hiding in the closet. Instead of being mad at him for messing around with his razor after repeated warnings to leave it alone, his father had used David's disobedience as a teachable moment. A moment that included both of them looking like Santa and laughing their fool heads off. Dad made everything fun. Even discipline for sin. What would his life have been like if he'd had to learn everything on his own? Terrified as he was now to learn about ministry without his father, he couldn't deny he'd already learned a ton just by watching the man.

There was a big difference in being on your own at eight years old and twenty-six. He'd had a father. A darn good one who loved him. A man who had forgiven him even without being asked.

David blinked back the gratitude welling in his eyes, but he didn't want to ever lose this incredible feeling that his father was watching him with a great deal of pleasure and silently urging him to give the same compassion he'd received.

David gently dragged the razor across Angus' tensed face. "See. It doesn't hurt, right?"

A smile cracked through the foam around Angus' mouth. "Tickles a little."

A strange mixture of delight and satisfaction came over David. For the first time, he understood his father's addiction to getting outside of himself and giving someone a hand up. "You give it a try."

Wide-eyed, Angus stood before the sink and took up the razor. Several shaky strokes later, Angus was the proud owner of a glistening face.

"Here." David stuck a piece of toilet paper to the small nick under Angus' chin. He stood back and admired the boy. "Good work, man." He clapped Angus on the back. "Ruthie Crouch won't know what hit her."

"Crouch?" Angus's voice cracked.

"Yeah, the lady who's graciously agreed to give you a shot at a real job." David mopped the counter. "Don't screw it up. You only get one chance to make a good first impression. Trust me. I know."

CHAPTER ELEVEN

"You may think your son's little civic project is harmless, Leona"—Maxine waved her condemning finger at Leona— "but I Googled missing teeth and I can tell you that homeless boy is a meth addict if I ever saw one."

Amy's jaw tightened as much in defense of Leona as Angus. "His drug tests came back negative."

Maxine wagged that same finger at Amy. "You'd do well to steer clear of this drugged-out vagrant too, young lady."

"He's sick, Maxine," Leona said.

"Says who? That new little doctor who treats us like we're all ignorant as fence posts?" Maxine tugged on the fur collar of her coat. "Well, I, for one, didn't fall off the turnip truck yesterday. I've watched enough of those reality cop specials to know druggies are good at snowing folks. They keep a spare bottle of sober pee in their pocket."

"That's ridiculous, Maxine," Amy argued. "Why would anyone do that?"

"It's for when they get hauled in. They can slip into the bathroom and just pour it into one of those little cups and no one is the wiser. In my educated opinion, you cannot trust those drug tests."

Amy gripped the spoon she'd been swirling through her coffee. "I drew his blood myself."

Undeterred by medical facts, Maxine turned to heap more of her displeasure on Leona. "When he steals you blind, don't think y'all are going to file a claim on the church insurance."

Amy sprang from her chair at the kitchen table where, until Maxine barged in unannounced, she'd been enjoying getting to know Leona while David was upstairs helping Angus clean up for his job interview. "Let he who is without sin cast the first stone."

Maxine put a hand to her chest like she'd taken a blow to the heart. "Voicing legitimate concerns is not casting stones."

Aunt Bette Bob had warned Amy to steer clear of this elder's wife, but Maxine had done nothing but criticize since she'd stormed into the Harper kitchen. Amy felt bad enough that she'd not said anything to defend the Harpers' privacy when she realized Maxine had let herself into the parsonage, but she drew the line at letting the slander of an innocent kid go unchallenged. "You're judging someone you don't even know."

"Leona, are you just going to stand there and let this outsider insult me in the very parsonage my contribution pays for?"

"Outsider?" Amy couldn't believe the nerve of this woman. "My mother grew up here. You went to school with her. I've lived in Mt. Hope over a year!"

"I think what Amy means, Maxine"—Leona's voice was far more placating than Amy thought the woman deserved—"Is that I'll pour you a cup of coffee and you can stick around and meet Angus." She offered the flustered elder's wife the chair Amy had vacated. "Once you get to know the boy, I'm sure you'll agree that he's a good kid who's simply had some very bad luck."

"You'll think bad luck when he murders y'all in your beds." Maxine reluctantly perched on the edge of the vinyl seat. "Cleaning up that mess would be a bigger job than getting up those hot chocolate and sugar cookie stains all those visitors leave on the sanctuary carpet after your little Christmas Eve services."

"Maxine, the boy has diabetes," Leona whispered, her head tilting toward David and Angus standing in the kitchen door. "He's not deaf."

"And I ain't dumb." Angus jammed his hands into the pockets of his new Walmart jeans.

"Oh, I believe you're very clever, young man." Maxine swiveled in her chair. "Choosing to pass out in our church proves you know how to play on the sympathies of good folks. It remains to be seen if you can prove yourself trustworthy."

"Maxine, the boy didn't choose to pass out in our fellowship hall," Leona snapped.

Amy couldn't help feeling a perverse pleasure at seeing Leona stand up to this horrible woman.

Maxine crossed her arms. "Maybe not, but—"

David interrupted, "Angus, let me introduce you to one of the members of Mt. Hope Community who has been praying for you." He took their lanky project by the elbow and urged him forward. "Right, Maxine?"

Maxine worked the words, "Of course, I've prayed for him," between her taut lips.

Angus flipped his wet hair out of his eyes. "Praying I leave town, most likely."

"Angus Freestone, I'd like you to meet Mrs. Howard Davis." David elbowed the boy in the ribs. "In the South we say, pleased to meet you."

Angus lifted his chin. "But I'm not pleased."

"Well, I can see you're suffering from a serious lack of upbringing, young man." Maxine snugged her purse under her crossed arms. "Davy, I know you young people have your ideas, after all Nellie's planning to put together a praise band for this year's Christmas Eve service. And let me tell you, Howard and I like that idea about as much as we like cookie crumbs on our pew, but I think taking in a stranger is unnecessarily dangerous."

"A praise band?" Leona's gaze shot to her son for an explanation. "For Christmas Eve?"

Maxine straightened in her seat. "Cornelia's planning the candlelight service this year, Leona. Didn't Davy tell you?"

"Momma." In an instant, David abandoned Angus and shot to his stiffened mother's side. Distress over the pain she wasn't able to conceal creased his brow. "I meant to tell you about Nellie's offer to take the burden off you this year, but it just slipped my mind."

Blinking the shock from her eyes, Leona whispered, "I've already arranged for Deacon Tucker to play Joseph."

"You ask Ivan to play Joseph every year, Leona," Maxine said.

"You're right, Maxine. I don't own the Christmas Eve service." Leona rallied a tight smile. "It was just another change I hadn't expected."

"See what I mean?" Maxine patted Leona's arm. "I thought with you elbow-deep in grief, this would be the perfect time to make a change."

"Change?" Leona's nostrils flared. "You've opposed every change J.D. ever suggested. If you wanted to *change* the Christmas Eve service why didn't you just ask me?"

Feeling responsible for the storm brewing in the kitchen, Amy leapt headfirst into the turbulence. She positioned herself between Angus and the two warring women. "Actually, Mrs. Harper, it's my fault David hasn't had a chance to talk to you. I recruited him to help with Angus, and I'm afraid finding Angus a job might have kept him a bit distracted."

"We cannot have a pastor so easily *distracted*," Maxine's barbs didn't stop there. She turned her threats on David and said, "I'm assuming your request for a special Board meeting means you want to become our permanent pastor. Am I right, Davy?"

David shook his head. "I'm willing to serve as an *interim,* if the church will have me."

"And Mt. Hope Community would be blessed to have him," Amy said. "Maxine, I heard you say how much you enjoyed his sermon."

"I've always loved Davy." Maxine's glare traveled between Amy and David, her knuckles white on the handle of her purse. "But, I can tell you right now, the members of Mt. Hope Community will not tolerate a pastor who champions drifters while the important affairs of the church, like the Christmas Eve service, languish."

"How can helping a man get a job be wrong, Maxine?" Indignation had transformed Leona's earlier surprise into fire and brimstone. "It's exactly the kind of work a pastor should be doing."

"Searching the Messenger's Help Wanted ads will suck Davy's time the same way it used to suck J.D.'s, and what will Davy have to show for the investment…a bunch of stacked up vagrants, that's what. Because let me tell you, word gets out we've helped one, they'll flock in faster than a gaggle of geese."

"Stacked up?" Instead of cowering, Leona took a bold step forward. "For your information, Angus already has a job. And it took *my boy* less than ten minutes to find it," Leona announced proudly.

"Your boy?" Maxine's eyes teared up. "Be glad you still have *your* boy."

"Maxine, I'm so sorry." Leona reached for the deflating woman. "I didn't mean to bring up—"

"You've always been glad it wasn't Davy on that horse that day." Cheeks streaked with tears, Maxine bolted past everyone.

Angus broke the silence. "Wow, I've seen people give up their last can of beans easier than you folks gave up on me."

Leona clapped both hands to her quivering mouth. Shaking her head in disbelief, she finally said, "I shouldn't have done that."

David wrapped his arm around his mother's shoulders. "Maxine and Howard are only two of the five votes on the Board, Momma. We're not down for the count yet."

"I shouldn't have pushed her," Leona insisted.

"She deserved it." Amy pulled out a chair and scooted it behind Leona. "It's about time someone put her in her place."

Leona sank onto the seat. "Maxine has suffered more than any woman ever should."

David kept his hand on his mother's shoulder and spoke gently to Amy, "Cornelia had a twin brother."

Amy's gut clenched. "Had?"

The rattle of the heater kicking on filled the strained silence. Finally, Angus said, "Man, you can't leave us hangin'. What happened to her boy?"

Leona cleared her throat. "Colton was sixteen and destined to be everything Maxine had ever dreamed. Smart. Handsome. Captain of the football team. World class barrel racer."

"And unlike Cornelia," David added. "Colt was great to be around. He and I spent every Sunday afternoon racing his horses. We dreamed of winning world champion barrel racer belt buckles. I just didn't have the horse. But Colt did."

"It was such a freak accident," Leona said, staring at nothing in particular.

Amy could see Leona was reliving whatever had happened as if it had happened to David. She held her breath, waiting for either David or Leona to finish the story.

Leona released a long, pained exhale. "Against Maxine's wishes, Howard bought Colton a very expensive Appaloosa. The horse was fast. Powerful. And very skittish." Leona swallowed. "But Colton assured her he could ride anything. And he could. Everyone knew that boy rode like he'd been born with a horse under him. Colton and his Appaloosa won every contest that year."

"They easily qualified for a spot at the World Championship," David added.

"So what happened?" Angus demanded.

"We all went to Oklahoma City to cheer him on. Even the Story sisters caught a bus and met us there," Leona began to painfully explain. "Colton had his horse warmed up and ready to enter the arena when someone in the stands honked one of those horrible air horns. Colton's spooked horse reared.

Maxine screamed for Colton to let go of the reins and jump." Leona clung to David's hand.

"But Colt would never leave his horse," David said quietly.

Leona drew a deep breath through her nose and let it out slowly as if the weight of this story sat squarely on her chest. "For a moment it looked as if Colton would regain control of the horse, but he couldn't. The arena footing was either too thin or too silty. No one knows for sure. Anyway, it doesn't matter. The Appaloosa toppled backwards. Colton's skull was crushed on impact." She paused for a second. "That sweet boy lingered a week before Howard finally convinced Maxine to let him go." Leona looked up, tears spilling from her eyes. "My best friend has never been the same."

Amy couldn't stop the flood of shame gliding down her own cheeks. Once again she'd judged someone without all the facts. "I didn't know Maxine was your best friend."

"Was," Leona said, softly.

CHAPTER TWELVE

Feeling as queasy as he did the day Colt died, David left the stunned nurse and his heartsick mother in the care of a vagrant and went to answer the doorbell. "Hey, Aunt Roxie."

The next-door neighbor stomped her boots on the mat. "Did I just see the Wicked Witch of the West peel out of here on her broom?"

"Momma set Maxine's hair on fire."

A pleased smile spread across Roxie's face. "That's a switch."

"Momma's not the same."

"No. She's not." Roxie's love wasn't limited to his mother. For years, she'd lavished her gifts of laughter and emotional support on the entire Harper family and whenever Aunt Roxie planted her feet, he knew she was gearing up to deliver another round of comfort. "I know this is hard for you David, but your mother will never be *that* woman again." Roxie reached up and took his face inside her gloved hands, sequestering his undivided attention. "But I have full confidence she'll emerge from this valley the strong, brave, bold woman God intended her to be. You hear me?"

David nodded. "Colton came up."

"I'm on it." Roxie plucked at her gloves. "Y'all leave your Momma to me."

Ten minutes later, David and Amy stepped into the cutting December wind with Angus in tow. David had offered to drive, but Amy said she needed some air. When she put her head down and set a brisk clip for the diner, David had no choice but to do his best to keep up.

After the first couple of blocks, Angus asked what he was going to get paid. David told him to be grateful for whatever Ruthie offered. Amy, on the other hand, hadn't said two words since she'd apologized for inciting the skirmish between Momma and Maxine. Maybe it was her medical training that propelled her into action whenever she saw people hurting, but remembering his ankle injury at camp, he knew it was something more. Empathy, warm and healing, oozed from this intriguing woman.

From the corner of his eye, David watched Amy replaying

the whole ugly scene again and again in her mind when suddenly something inside him changed. Everything he'd thought he wanted in the past—financial security, prestige, an escape from life in the parsonage—shriveled and fell away. All he could see when he looked at this beautiful girl walking beside him was what he wanted now. Someone who believed in him. Someone who believed there was good in people. Someone whose desire to help others matched his own growing desire to make a difference.

Knowing he couldn't settle for allowing their relationship to stall out at friendship, he reached for Amy's hand. "Stop beating yourself up." To his relief, she didn't pull away. "I've tried to figure out what happened between Momma and Maxine for years."

"I've been thinking..."

"Uh-oh," David teased, trying to lighten her pensive mood. "Last time you did some thinking, I ended up a surrogate parent to a teenager."

"I ain't deaf, remember?" Angus said from a few steps behind them.

"Or dumb," David shot back, in hopes teasing Angus might ease Amy's frown. "And it's *I'm not* deaf, not *ain't* deaf." He squeezed Amy's hand. "I may regret this, but I want to hear what you've been thinking."

She stared straight ahead, weighing her words carefully. "Sometimes when grief gets redirected, the feelings of loss and sadness can morph into anger. Maxine is still mad."

"At what? That I'm alive and Colton's not? I've known that for ten years."

"I think it's more than that. Maxine's mad her life dreams died while your mother's progressed naturally."

"If you want to count losing your best friend and then your husband as an enviable progression, then I guess you're right."

"Both of Leona's kids grew up. Maddie's going to be a doctor." Amy's grip tightened. "And Colton's best friend, whom Maxine loved like a son, not only listens to his mother, he's become a fine man who, without a moment's hesitation, completely and unselfishly devoted his life to getting his mother back on her feet."

"Colton would have done the same thing for his mother if the tables had been turned."

"Maybe. Maybe not. I'm not saying Maxine's thinking is rational. Grief-born anger seldom is. I know from experience that we don't mean to hurt those we love when we're grieving. It's just that they are the ones most likely to stick close."

"And that makes them easy targets."

"Your Mom doesn't take Maxine's jabs because she's

afraid she's going to lose the parsonage."

He stopped. "She's afraid of losing Maxine."

"As long as Maxine's still punching, your mother can hope she'll either wear out or let her anger go," Amy whispered. "And when she does, your momma is the kind of woman who'll be there with her arms open."

Had Amy always been so wise or was this a skill she'd gained through her struggle? "I'm not proud of some of the things I've said to you and yet, here you are. What does that mean for us?"

Amy caught a glimpse of the desire he hadn't tried to hide. Her breath sputtered out in little white clouds. "David, I can't—"

"Hey!" Angus tapped David on the shoulder. "I didn't take a shower and shave to watch this sappy Hallmark movie. You two need to either get a room or take me to this job interview."

A hint of a smile tugged Amy's mouth. "Guess we'll have to solve the world's problems on our own time."

David hooked his arm around her waist and pulled her close. "Or maybe we should kiss and really gross the boy out?"

Her laugh was musical. He could only imagine how wonderful it would be to hear her sing.

As he started to ask her about singing at the Christmas

Eve service, Amy gently pushed back. "Angus has had enough gory details for one day."

Maybe Angus had seen enough, but David knew he'd do anything to see her laugh in his arms again.

The lunch crowd had thinned out by the time the three of them walked under the jangling bell above the diner door.

"Ruthie, we've got your new waiter," David announced.

The diner owner stopped wiping the counter. Her gaze jumped straight to the tall boy standing beside David. She grabbed her chest. "He's got my Ruby's eyes," tumbled from her quivering lips.

CHAPTER THIRTEEN

"How do you know my mom's name?" Angus stormed toward Ruthie.

Amy rushed to stop the boy from leaping over the counter. "Let her explain, Angus."

Ruthie planted both palms on the Formica, bracing herself. "Ruby was my girl. Did she tell you about me?"

"She said I had a grandmother in Mt. Hope. She never told me your name or where to find you. But I seen her maiden name on this birth certificate." He pulled a folded piece of paper from his pocket and thrust it across the counter. "Here. Proves I ain't a liar."

Ruthie carefully unfolded the certificate and read it slowly. She laid the paper on the counter. When she looked up, tears trickled down her cheeks. "I wish I could have been there when you were born." Ruthie swallowed. "But your momma and I didn't part on the best of terms."

"Mom said you were hard, but fair."

Ruthie gave a little shrug. "I had big plans for Ruby and this place." She waved her hand over the empty diner. "I dreamed of expanding this greasy spoon into a fine dining establishment, with linen tablecloths, real china, and a fold-out menu. But all Ruby dreamed about was expanding her horizons. She wanted out of this one-horse town real bad. So bad, she went and got herself pregnant by some trucker." Ruthie brushed a hand across her wet cheeks. "For the last seventeen years, I've been wishing I'd been more fair and less hard." She looked Angus square in the face. "You think she could ever forgive me?"

"No."

Ruthie swallowed. "Guess I deserve that."

"She's dead."

Ruthie's hand clutched at the buttons on her blouse. "Dead?"

"Ruthie?" Amy flew around the counter. "David, help me get her to a stool."

David hooked his arm through Ruthie's and helped Amy guide her around the bar.

Once they had Ruthie perched atop a stool, she waved

them off and asked Angus, "How she'd die? When?"

"Overdosed. Six months ago."

Ruthie squeezed her eyes shut. "I told her to leave that stuff alone." Tears she did not try to hide slid down her cheeks. "But she couldn't hear me over the demons that had her in their claws." Anger pushed her remorse aside. "And that no good dad of yours just left you on your own?"

"He died when I was eight. Mom did her best to keep a roof over our heads. Said if her mom could raise a kid alone, how hard could it be?"

Ruthie's lips quivered. "How did you get here, boy?"

"Walked."

"From where?"

"Maine."

"You walked half-way across the country?"

"Had nothin' else to do. Nowhere else to go."

"You don't need nowhere else. You're home." Ruthie opened her arms. "Come to your MeMaw, boy."

Angus fell into her embrace.

Joy tingled throughout Amy's body. She felt David's arm slip around her shoulder. As he hugged her close, she couldn't help but turn into him.

"We did it," his whispered excitement warmed her cheek.

"We did." The same profound awe coursing through her

body glistened in his eyes. Together, they'd orchestrated this incredible prodigal homecoming. Together, they'd been the hands and feet of Jesus. Together, they'd helped make a difference in two people's lives.

Overwhelming joy awakened Amy's desire to belong, to be loved by someone special, desires she'd buried after her diagnosis. Desires she'd laid to rest alongside every physical desire ripping through her now. She wanted to be loved…and she wanted to be loved by this man.

Before she could remind herself of her commitment to a celibate life, Amy flung her arms around David's neck and kissed him square on the mouth. Not the soft, sweet kiss she'd imagined, but a kiss filled with surprising urgency.

David's arms encircled her in an instant, drawing her tight against him. What she'd intended as a peck of gratitude quickly deepened and before she knew it, nothing else mattered.

CHAPTER FOURTEEN

Amy and David lingered outside as twilight settled over the diner, neither of them in a hurry to break the magical spell. Under the blinking light of the Koffee Kup's neon sign, they stood shoulder to shoulder watching the touching scene of Ruthie proudly introducing Angus to the regulars who'd gathered around the bar.

David's fingers intertwined with hers. "We do good work, don't we?" Satisfaction beamed from his smile in an intimate tilt of his lips meant just for her. The taste of those lips lingered on hers. He leaned over and whispered in her ear, "Harper and Maxwell Incorporated. Shall we make our partnership official?"

She turned. His head was bent toward hers. His lips poised to kiss her again. She would never forget the delicious tingle of his mouth pressed against her own.

However, she couldn't afford to confuse one impetuous kiss with true desire for a deeper relationship. Looking into his hopeful eyes, she knew it would be easier to deny her part in David's happiness than to deny how it thrilled her heart to have a small part in helping this man find his true purpose.

But treating him like a rescue kitten was wrong. David didn't need her. He was a smart guy. Eventually, he would figure out who he was on his own. After all, she'd worked through her grief and adjusted to a life of self-sufficiency, he would too.

The struggle would make him stronger, and she wouldn't be tempted to give the desires his nearness aroused a foothold. It was natural to feel euphoric after the scene they'd just witnessed, she reasoned, but in order to break away from the attraction that kept pulling her toward this man, she'd have to do what she'd been trained to do, the hardest part of nursing. She had to walk away before a patient she cared about was totally on his feet.

She extricated her hand from his. "We did."

"Wait." He grabbed her arm and snugged her up against him. "I know you want to do it again," he teased. "Come on, admit it."

She knew he was asking for more than helping orphaned

boys find their families. He was asking her to kiss him again. "We'll both find our ways to serve the community."

Recoiling as if she'd slapped him, David moved her to arms' length. "Just not together?"

"Friends help each other no matter what, right?"

"Didn't *you* just kiss *me*?" The pressure he applied to her arms betrayed his attempt to keep the discussion light.

"I got swept up in the moment."

He moved forward and took both of her hands in his. "Then let's go save someone else because I want to kiss you again. And again. And again."

"Whoa, cowboy." She pulled free. "Remember we're just friends."

A seductive grin activated his dimples. "According to Momma, friends make the best lovers."

"That's not happening."

"Why not?"

Opening up was too dangerous. She was private. She'd spent her whole life trying to keep her condition under wraps. It had been exhausting when she was young, but keeping her secret now, when she longed to trust someone with the truth, required a hundred times more effort.

"Because pastors who take on lovers usually get fired."

"I don't want *lovers*." David's persistent approach invaded her personal space.

Trapped between his lithe, muscular body and the diner window, she had no choice but to try and silence her wildly beating heart and listen to this man on a mission.

"I want a wife." His hands cupped her face. The soft caress of his dark brown eyes sank into her soul. "I want you, Amy Maxwell."

For one gut-wrenching second, she wavered between David and a less lonely life. Could a future with someone other than a cat actually be possible for her? The blare of a car horn barreling down Main startled her back to reality.

Fighting the rush of anxiety engulfing her, Amy removed his hands and pressed herself against the cold bricks. "I can't marry anyone. Ever."

"Why?"

Once she told him her whole story, she could never take it back, but from his determined face she wasn't going to get away with keeping her secret to herself. "I can't have children." Whispered words. Stabbing knives. "Ever."

"Who said?" He wasn't grasping the significance of what she was trying to tell him, and apparently there was no working it out in his mind because he asked again, "Who would dare tell a woman that?"

"Experts."

"What kind of experts?"

"Teams and teams of diabetic specialists." She wrapped her arms around her barren middle to keep her heart from bleeding out. "I was diagnosed with juvenile diabetes when I was two."

As the truth sunk in, his charming grin took on a cavalier defiance. "So?"

"So … no matter how well all of those doctors tried to manage my disease, years of unstable glucose levels have taken a toll on my organs. That's why Angus has to be so careful, but at least he can father children without putting his body at risk. If I happen to get pregnant, the strain could kill me."

David clasped her shoulders, his eyes swimming with compassion. "Did I say I wanted a bunch of kids, or did I say I wanted you?"

"See, this is why any girl could fall in love with you." Tears made it hard to speak. "You're selfless."

"No, I'm not. I'm a selfish pig. I'm preaching so I don't have to take care of my mother for the rest of her life. I'm helping Angus so that I can preach. And, most selfish of all, I want you. No matter what. Just you."

Amy gave a little shake of her head. "You may think you can live without kids now, but I've seen how you really are.

With Angus. You love him. You'll make a terrific father and someday you're going to want a son of your own. Then you'll look at me and ... and I won't be able to stand the disappointment in your eyes."

"You're going to have to trust me, Amy."

"Trust? Isn't that the pot calling the kettle black? You don't trust anybody. Especially not yourself." She pushed him away. "Don't call me again." She ran and didn't look back.

CHAPTER FIFTEEN

Silently cursing the wind, the darkness, and his inability to comfort the woman he loved, David spun in the opposite direction and crashed smack into the brickhouse attorney his father had hired behind everyone's back.

"Where's the fire?" From Saul's planted legs and open stance, this was a lawyer not easily flustered.

"Sorry, Mr. Levy," David backed away, palms in the air.

"I'm closed for the night." Saul aimed his laser gaze between David's eyes. "If you're finally coming around to see what I had to say, you'll have to make an appointment."

"Excuse me?"

"Sent you two texts today. Never heard back."

"I didn't get any texts." David pulled out his phone. Sure enough, in the flurry of getting Angus settled, he'd let Saul's messages go unanswered. Heat creeping up his neck, David lowered his phone. "I've been a little busy."

Saul neither grinned nor gloated. He simply said, "Guess that frees me up to work directly with your mother?"

"Technically, it doesn't. I'm her counsel."

"Then act like it, boy." Saul strode past him and pushed his way into the diner.

David crammed his phone back into his pocket, lowered his head against the wind, and stalked toward home. He was failing on every front. Failing to help his mother sort through whatever legal mess left by his father. Failing to ease the tension between his mother and Maxine, putting Momma's ability to remain in the home she adored in even greater danger. Failing to fill his father's shoes. Sunday was coming and he hadn't started his sermon, let alone assembled the persuasive arguments he'd need when he met with the Board to gain his interim approval. And finally, most frustrating of all, he'd failed to offer any kind of defense when Amy accused him of being incapable of trusting anyone, especially himself. If he couldn't trust himself, how could he expect her to trust him when he said he didn't want kids?

Kids?

Did he want them? He hadn't intentionally put children on his list of life's goals. But neither had he crossed off fatherhood as part of his very distant future.

Hadn't Saul just proved he wasn't mature enough to take care of himself and his mother? He didn't need a houseful of kids. If it came down to a choice between Amy as his wife or a woman fertile as a guppy, Amy would win hands down. Because what he wanted, no, needed, was a woman who centered him. Without Amy in his life, he could see himself wandering from school to school, adding degrees to his resume, and never finding his true purpose. And for once, that sounded awful.

The bass thrum of loud music blasted David from his dire reflections and projections. He looked up and found himself standing outside the front doors of Mt. Hope Community Church. He didn't remember walking the six blocks between the diner and the church, but here he was. Yellow light spilled from the vibrating stained-glass windows.

"What the heck?" Fingers numb from the cold, David fumbled with his keys. By the time he stepped into the building, every bone in his body rattled. A deep bass rhythm pumped from the sanctuary. He crossed the foyer and opened the door to the usually dark and quiet auditorium.

David scanned the unbelievable scene.

On the lit-up stage, Wilma Wilkerson, the church organist, stood behind an electronic keyboard. Her eyes were closed and her beefy hands were flying over the keys. He traced the throb in his clenched jaw to Amy's Aunt Bette Bob who was rockin' out on an electric guitar. Ivan Tucker pounded the mammoth drum set spread across the back of the stage. Front and center, Nellie Davis pranced before two freestanding spotlights. She sang with her closed eyes and both hands wrapped around the handheld microphone plastered to her bottom lip.

Nellie was so engrossed in belting out the words to a gravelly country version of *Hark the Herald Angels Sing* she didn't notice David charging down the aisle, his arms waving frantically and shouting, "Nellie, what is God's name is going on?" Ivan's nerve-shattering bang to a cymbal swallowed David's objections whole.

Determined to put a stop to this foolishness, David marched to the stage lip and yanked the overloaded power strip from the socket. Silence fell over the sanctuary.

Nellie's eyes popped open, her claws ready to tear into whoever had shut her down. "David?" She noticed the cords dangling from the surge protector still in his hand. "You could have waited to the end of the song to thank us."

"Nellie, what is *this*?" He waved the power strip over the stage.

"It's *Cornelia*," she corrected. "And *this* is my Christmas

Eve praise band."

"Praise band?"

"The one we talked about, remember?"

"We agreed to a few Christmas songs. Not a country western hoedown. And what happened to asking Amy Maxwell to sing?"

Nellie turned to her band. "While David and I iron out our little creative differences, why don't y'all take five?"

Bette Bob's eyebrows shot up. "Why didn't you invite my niece to sing, Nellie?"

"Cornelia," Nellie corrected as she laid her mic down. "I needed the instruments up to speed before I brought on more vocalists, Bette Bob."

"Come on Wilma and Ivan." Bette Bob undid her guitar strap. "I may have brownies in the oven and coffee brewing in the fellowship hall, but I know stink cabbage when I smell it."

Once the band exited the auditorium, Nellie came down off the stage. "David, you really need to work on your people skills, especially when you're dealing with volunteers. They're temperamental."

"For your information, my people skills are just fine."

"Is that why my mother asked my father to vote against your interim proposal?"

David's anger rumbled in his gut. "Don't try to blackmail

me, Nell."

She flinched at his refusal to call her Cornelia. "Look, you took on Amy's little social experiment, not me."

"Leave Amy out of it."

The moment the words left his mouth, Nellie's keen radar flashed in her green eyes. She'd picked up on his passion for the blonde nurse and he was going to pay. A slow, Cheshire grin spread across Nellie's perfect teeth. David instinctively tightened the scarf around his neck.

"You know what?" Nellie purred. "I should let you sink, drown in your own stubborn stupidity. But, in case you haven't noticed, I've loved you too long to let you fail now." She swallowed her hurt and quickly continued, "So, here's what we're going to do. I'm going to work with this band until they sparkle, and you're going to keep my parents happy by letting me do this for you." As she brushed past him, she purposefully grazed her tightly-sweatered breasts against his arm. She plucked her coat from the front pew. "Be a dear and turn off the lights on your way back to your precious parsonage."

"When hell freezes over."

"Remember, David." Nellie pivoted slowly. "Board members are the most temperamental of all volunteers." She threw her coat over her shoulder as easily as she tossed around ugly threats and sashayed out.

Power strip clutched in his hand, David shook the tangled mess of cords at the empty pulpit. He'd been a fool to think he could fill his father's shoes. "I can't do this, God. I thought I could. But I can't."

Why hadn't he listened to his grandmother and taken over his grandfather's firm?

Wait.

He wasn't married to this place, and Amy had made it abundantly clear he would never be married to her. There was nothing holding him here. His law license was still current. Once he took over the firm, he could afford to move Momma anywhere she wanted to go. She'd always wanted to travel and he'd have the financial means to make that happen. Seeing the world would help her see her precious parsonage for what it was...a smothering glass dome over her head. And he'd make it his mission in life to see that his mother got over Howard and Maxine Davis.

They'd gotten over her a long time ago.

"David?"

He turned. "Momma?" His mother stood at the back of the sanctuary, the afghan one of the Story sisters had crocheted for her wrapped around her shoulders. "What are you doing coming into the building by yourself this late at night? It's dangerous."

"Apparently." Her eyes moved past him and on to the stage. "What's all that?"

He sighed. "Nellie's brainchild."

Momma strode the aisle, the afghan flowing behind like a crusader's cape. "Her praise band."

"Yep."

"Are they any good?"

"Momma, what difference does it make? They're not playing."

"Why not?"

"You and I both know the moment Ivan bangs that drum, half of the congregation will walk out."

Her eyes narrowed. "James David Harper, what have you done?"

"I told Nellie to take her band and—"

Momma held up her palm. "And she told you…what?"

He sighed and dropped onto the front pew. "Momma, aren't you tired of kowtowing to every holier-than-thou thug in this church?"

Momma motioned for him to scoot over. "None of us get to have our own way all the time." She picked up the hymnal with Parker Kemp's last song list peeking out from the yellowed pages. "Maxine may grouse about my traditional

Christmas Eve program but she doesn't want a praise band. She loves singing those old hymns and carols." Momma pulled out Parker's list. "See. These are Maxine's song selection *suggestions* for next week. Not a single song on her playlist was written before the Revolutionary War. Parker throws her a bone and sings a couple of her suggestions each week. Seems to make her happy."

"So why did she agree to this?" He flicked his wrist at the collection of instruments on the stage.

"Maxine wants the same thing I want." Momma smiled at him, tears glistening in her eyes. "Her child's happiness."

He studied this tower of strength sitting beside him. Who was she and what happened to the woman who'd trained him to jump in and save her before he saved himself if the family van ever went over a bridge? "Amy says it's not the parsonage you're hanging on to, but the hope that one day you and Maxine will be friends again."

"Wise girl, your Amy."

"She's not *my* Amy, Momma."

"Could have fooled me, and most people don't." She patted his knee. "Come on, I smell Bette-Bob brownies in the kitchen."

"I've had a belly-full for one night."

"Of Nellie?"

"Of vagrants. Church politics. Women. Everything."

Momma didn't ask about Angus or the boy's job interview. She didn't even ask why Amy wasn't here with him. Instead, she said, "David, you can either be the mesquite thorn that flattens tires, or you can be an olive branch for hurting souls." She lifted his chin. "The choice has always been yours."

"Let me guess…J.D. Harper's dying words?"

"No." Momma's gaze slid up to the empty pulpit that had been pushed aside to make room for the band. "Your father lived with a willingness to always put himself in someone else's shoes."

"And, by implication, Dad would want me to look at this from Nellie's point of view?"

"More than anything, your father wanted this church to live with an open heart, to grow in their ability to look beyond themselves."

David blew out a long slow breath. "Saul Levy wants to see us."

Momma sighed and eased back against the pew. "It can wait until after Christmas, can't it?" She nodded toward the stage. "I think it's going to be a good show this year."

David laid a heavy hand on hers. "It can wait, Momma."

CHAPTER SIXTEEN

The next morning, Shirley trailed David to his father's office and shut the door. "Have you seen what that Davis girl has done to the sanctuary?"

"Yep."

"You're not letting her get away with it, are you?"

"Nope."

"That explains the phone call I got from Etta May." Thankfully, Shirley wasn't one to make him work for the point of a conversation. "She wanted me to warn you that a considerable number of naysayers have joined Maxine's campaign to keep Mt. Hope Community ... vagrant-free."

"Angus isn't a vagrant." David tossed his computer bag on the desk. "The kid's an orphan who came in search of his widowed grandmother. If this church isn't willing to help widows and orphans, maybe I'm wasting my time here and Mt. Hope Community should shut its doors."

Shirley peered over her glasses. "You're preachin' to the choir, you know?"

David dropped into his father's desk chair. He dragged his hand over the stubble he'd left on his face in defiance of Nellie's attempts to make him into someone he wasn't. "Maybe it's time I preached the hard truth to the entire church."

"I'm not saying Maxine wouldn't benefit from a strong dose of scripture, but are you sure that's the tactic you want to take?"

"There's more, isn't there?"

Chewing on the corner of her lip, Shirley nodded. "It's not good."

"Let me guess. Maxine wants my name removed from interim pastor consideration." David set back in his father's wobbly chair. "What would Dad do, Shirley?"

"You're not your daddy."

Come Sunday morning, David had never felt that truth more. He stood on the front row, shifting foot to foot as Parker Kemp wrapped up the last song on Maxine's suggested list.

Parker had tried to explain before the worship service that he wasn't taking sides, but he wasn't going to throw gas on the smoldering embers. "What will it hurt to sing a few of Maxine's favorites?"

Everything. That's what.

Maxine's days of nailing Harpers with the sledge hammer of grief she'd carried around for ten years had to end. After all, Maxine wasn't the only one who'd suffered since Colton died. David lost his best friend that day and Momma lost hers.

The moment Parker asked everyone to be seated David took his exasperation to the podium.

He planted his father's shoes behind his father's pulpit. He opened his father's Bible, but he took out his own notes. His tongue was a coiled whip of scriptures he'd spent hours preparing. Channeling the image of Jesus clearing the temple, David believed the time had come to unleash some righteous anger. He raised his eyes and aimed for Maxine and Howard. Nellie sat beside them, her shining auburn hair a reminder he was playing with fire. Three birds. One stone.

He had nothing to lose. If the Harpers were going down in flames, at least he could hold his head up and know he hadn't let Momma down without a fight.

A hymnal smacked the wooden floor beneath the pews. Everyone jumped then turned to see who had been so careless.

Angus? In church. Without being forced since he'd moved

out of the parsonage and in with his grandmother. And he'd brought Ruthie with him.

David had forgotten all about the invitation he'd extended them that night in the diner. He couldn't believe they'd accepted. The kid, red hair slicked down and a red flush creeping up from the stiff white collar buttoned around his neck, sat deer-in-the-headlights still beside his equally uncomfortable grandmother. Angus's guilty eyes darted back and forth, searching for a way of escape from the unwanted attention. Amy, sitting on the other side of Angus, patted the boy's hand reassuringly. She mouthed, *it's okay*, then bent, scooped up the songbook, and slid it quietly into the rack on the back of Maxine's pew.

Amy.

David's gaze locked with Amy's. He hadn't expected to see her here either. He'd reached out to her several times these past few days, but she'd not returned his calls or texts.

Sunlight lit the golden curls framing Amy's beautiful, yet very neutral face. He had no idea what she was thinking. Was she an angel sent to offer support? Or was she here as the innocent victim of his unwanted affections intent on seeing him hanged?

Momma's admonition to be an olive branch rather than a mesquite thorn rang in his ears.

No way.

He straightened his notes and cleared his throat. Tiny actions, but as his father used to say, tiny actions were the wheels that set the greatest actions in motion. To his surprise, when he looked up, his cloud of anger had lifted and he could finally see what his father must have seen every time he took this pulpit.

Before him sat a group of good people. People he'd known most of his life. People who loved him as much as they loved this church. People who would themselves be living on the fringe had they not found this place to belong. People he could trust.

His eyes found Amy's. A twinge lifted the corner of her lip.

David stuffed his notes under his father's Bible and took a breath. Instead of the tirade he'd prepared, a verse his father had taught him years ago flowed from his lips. "Let us continue to love one another, for love comes from God." As he emphasized the word *love,* he noticed Amy swallow hard. "...for God is love."

Silence hung over the sanctuary.

David inched the toe of his father's shoe against the stool hidden beneath the pulpit, the stool he and his father had built for David's first sermon. "J.D. Harper was a man who loved. When I look out across this auditorium, I know my father learned the meaning of sacrificial and unconditional love from you."

David scanned the crowd, letting his gaze fall upon Etta May and Nola Gay. These two shriveled up women had parked themselves on his parents' couch every Sunday morning for as long as he could remember. They were quirky, nosey, and opinionated but generous to a fault.

He took a breath. "For years, some have used their gift of generosity to cover the contribution shortfalls. Not out of abundance, but rather a generosity of spirit. Widow's mites offered in faith." The older twins shifted in their seats, blushing at his praise.

David let his gaze drift to Amy's aunt. "Some have used their gift of hospitality. No one in Mt. Hope comes down with a cold, has a baby, or goes home from the hospital without a full-course meal and lots of delicious chocolate." Everyone knew exactly who he was talking about, including Bette Bob who was suddenly very interested in the floorboards. "And this same quiet servant has even opened her home." His gaze paused on Amy. Her smile of understanding was gas to his fire.

David turned to the owner of the local paper, the man who'd hired him as a scrawny teenager to throw papers and had now hired his mother as a journalist. "And then there are those who take chances and give job opportunities to those who don't deserve it."

Momma glowed from her place on the front row. But David couldn't stop there.

His gaze honed in on Maxine and instead of anger he felt compassion. "There are some who've had many reasons to leave." The elder's wife stiffened. "To move their membership and take their significant contributions with them. But they've stayed at Mt. Hope Community. Why? Because this church is their family. They love us." He stopped short of saying, prickles and all, when he noticed tears streaming down Maxine's face. "And we love them."

David wrapped his hands around the edge of the pulpit. "I confess I'm not my father. Loving unconditionally does not come easily to me. Growing up as the preacher's kid I often felt like I was living under a magnifying glass." David smiled, the first real smile he'd offered these people since his first sermon atop the stool. "But I've finally learned what my father knew all along about this church and the people who fill these pews...you see all my faults, but you love me anyway...encouraging me through my struggles."

David reached beneath the pulpit and pulled out his old step stool. "You accepted me when I chose the law rather than the pulpit. You cheered me on when I wandered from the law to studying history. And when I came busting back in here, determined to save my parents' life work, you clapped me on the back and told me to have at it."

Fighting a wave of emotion, David ran his fingers over the name his father had carved in the stool. *David.* "It is because I have experienced your unconditional love, I know it is possible for you to love everyone the Lord sends through our doors...even those on the fringe. Love like this is salt. And there's a hungry world out there. Forgive me for daring to think you would let them starve." He slid the stool back in place, then closed his father's Bible. "Next Sunday, I hope you'll not only join us for a special Christmas Eve service, but invite your friends. Nellie's band will rock the house." Bible in hand, he descended the steps of the stage, stopped at the front pew, and offered Momma his arm.

She smiled like he was a rock star and slipped her hand through the crook in his elbow. Together they walked toward the sanctuary doors to face whatever came next.

CHAPTER SEVENTEEN

Amy hung back, her heart aching as she watched each member hugging David before they filed out of the sanctuary. She'd never admired this church more. Nor did she think it possible to love this selfless man any more than she did at this very moment. David hated making himself vulnerable, and yet he'd trusted his feelings to the very people he'd felt had judged him. And she knew why.

He'd meant it when he said he wanted this church to grow. And he wanted it to grow in more than attendance numbers. He wanted Mt. Hope Community to become everything his father believed possible. He longed to make a difference in this world as much as she.

Her heart was torn between wishing David's version of unconditional love hadn't so blatantly included her and knowing she couldn't let David throw his newfound love for this church away. He had so much to give. To this town. To these people. To a woman who could give him the family he deserved.

David's eyes met hers over the crowd of people surrounding him. His smile, the intimate one she'd seen after their kiss, beckoned her to come to him…unconditionally. Her heart pushed every argument from her head. If he could learn to trust, couldn't she? She stepped into the aisle and bumped into Nellie.

"Sorry, Nellie. I—"

"It's Cornelia." Cornelia started to say something else but was cut off by a wave of coughing. She snagged Amy's arm indicating she wanted her to wait. When the torture of listening to each raspy hack subsided, Nellie whispered, "I've been meaning to …"—she cleared her throat, flipped her hair over her shoulder, exposing her long, slender neck—"call you."

"Call *me*? Why?"

"David and I had a long chat over dinner the other night about the Christmas Eve program I've been rehearsing and—"

"Dinner?"

"More of a date, really." Nellie's voice was hoarse and gravelly. Probably from the same long, late-night rehearsals that were also taking a toll on Aunt Bette Bob. "Anyway,"—

Nellie dug through her large Gucci purse—"I promised David I'd ask you to sing *Mary Did You Know* at the Christmas Eve show." She pulled out a piece of sheet music. "Here's the arrangement we're using. Rehearsal tonight. Here. At five."

She wanted to ask why Nellie had waited until it was far too late to master this difficult song, but instead she asked, "Nellie, how long have you had that lump at the base of your throat?"

Nellie's hand flew to her neck. "A month. Maybe two."

"*Two months* and you haven't had it checked?"

"I've been busy, okay?"

"No. It's not," Amy said. "Is your throat sore?"

"Well, sure. I've been singing every night trying to get ready for Christmas."

"Sore as in strep-throat-kind-of-sore or more of an achy pain?"

"Pain, okay?"

"Any problems swallowing?"

"Look, you're a nurse. Not a doctor. I'm fine."

Amy looked Nellie square in the eyes. "I think you should have it checked." Over Nellie's shoulder Amy caught David's brown-eyed gaze. His smile was a lifeline she would miss if she wasted another minute arguing with someone who clearly didn't want her advice. "But your health is your business." She started toward David, but Nellie angled her body and cut Amy off from the man waiting for her at the sanctuary doors.

"Your sudden concern has nothing to do with my health, does it?" Nellie pinned Amy to the end of the pew. "You're trying to put me out so you can steal my show, aren't you?"

"I'm not stealing anything." Amy thrust the music back at Nellie. "I'm not singing."

An evil twinkle flashed in Nellie's eyes. "Oh, I get it." She rolled the sheet music and poked Amy's shoulder with it. "You're mad because David needs a girl like me to get him where he wants to go. You think I've stolen your chance to live happily ever after with the new pastor in the parsonage."

Amy glanced at David again, but he was no longer looking at her. The Story sisters had diverted his attention. Flanked by his mother, David was laughing, enjoying the members of Mt. Hope Community like she'd never seen him do before. He was at home.

Mother. Loyal, loving son. And the hope of future generations.

Suddenly a sad image washed over Amy. David was standing alone at her grave. There were no children to support him in his grief. No future generations offering hope. Had she heard what she wanted to hear during his sermon? Could David really be happy without a family? Believing she would be enough for any man was like believing in Christmas miracles.

Amy pushed the music away. "You can't take what I never had." She wheeled.

Instead of going into the arms of the man she loved, she hurried to the other end of the pew.

From the corner of her eye she saw David coming for her. "Amy."

Before he could reach her, she cut right and headed for the back door and the lonely role she'd accepted long before Nellie Davis took the stage.

CHAPTER EIGHTEEN

David could have sworn the smile Amy had given him during his sermon meant his willingness to trust the congregation with his feelings had broken through her crazy barriers. Then, after church, when their eyes connected across the crowded sanctuary, he knew his message had gotten through. One minute she was making her way toward him, the next she was running the opposite direction. If he didn't know better, he could have sworn Nellie had something to do with Amy's disappearance, but when he'd questioned Nellie, she claimed she didn't know what happened. All she'd done was offer Amy a plum song, which Amy had thrown back in her face.

He had to confess he'd been a bit surprised that Nellie had actually done what he'd asked and invited Amy to sing, but then Nellie had surprised him on many levels. She'd transformed Mt. Hope Community's ragtag band into something pretty decent. She'd given him a detailed list of everything that had to be done, programs, decorating, refreshments, etc., which was great since he had no idea how to put on a Christmas Eve service and he didn't want to burden his mother. But Nellie had even convinced him to let her ask his mother to help with some of the decorating. He could see the need to be needed had done Momma a world of good.

He'd given Amy a couple of days and several missed phone calls to explain. He checked his phone again. Not one reply to all the calls and texts he'd sent. Angus had let it slip that Amy planned to drop by the Koffee Kup and help him get enrolled in school. David threw on his jacket and set out for the diner. He intended to camp out in the back booth until she showed.

The bell above the diner door jangled.

Angus looked up from behind the counter, an incriminating grin on his face. "Hey, David. Just put on a fresh pot of coffee. Want some?"

David covertly scanned the diner for signs of a certain blonde. His hopes sank. No sign of Amy. He didn't want to tip Angus off by asking if he'd missed her. "Is your coffee safe to drink?"

"He makes the best coffee you'll ever have." Ruthie swiveled around on one of the bar stools. "Only had to show this boy how to operate the Bunn one time and"—she snapped her fingers—"he had it down pat."

"I did most of the cookin' for me and Mom." Angus scratched his head. "But it's a little different cookin' for a crowd."

"He's a natural," Ruthie bragged. She leaned in and whispered, "Did you know a sprinkle of salt over dry coffee grounds keeps the brew from getting bitter?"

David sat on the stool next to Ruthie. "I did not."

"Me neither," Ruthie said. "I'm telling you, my grandson is a sharp one."

"Awe, MeMaw." Angus set a steaming mug in front of David. "She always go on and on like that?"

David lifted his cup. "Ruthie's usually more generous with her fries than her praise."

"People can change," Ruthie said.

"I'm counting on it." David took a sip. "Coffee does taste better with a hint of salt."

"Which brings up something I've been meaning to ask you." Angus put his elbows on the counter and planted his head in his hands, his face very serious. "You know how you talked about being salt Sunday?"

"What about it?"

"Can anybody be salt?"

"Absolutely."

"Good." Angus smiled. "I've been thinking…I'm real grateful for all you and the folks at Mt. Hope Community did for me."

"Makes us happy to see you so happy, Angus." David took another swig.

"I want to be salt," Angus said, firmly.

David blew coffee everywhere. "You do?" He'd never expected his preaching to actually change someone.

"What the boy is trying to say"—Ruthie ripped napkins from the holder and mopped up David's mess—"Can anybody be part of Mt. Hope Community or do you have to be somebody special to join up?"

"You are somebody special, Ruthie," David said. "And we'd love for you to join us. In fact, I could use some help."

"What do you need?" Ruthie chucked the wet napkins in a bin behind the counter. "You name it."

"You sure Angus isn't too busy with school?" David asked fishing for info on Amy.

"Amy signed him up yesterday, but the principal said he might as well wait until after the first of the year to get going."

Trying not to let his disappointment show, David said,

"Okay then. Bette Bob usually comes to the church on Christmas Eve day to make all the brownies for the refreshments after the service," David said. "But the band will be rehearsing right up to the time we open the doors. Know any good cooks?"

Angus grinned. "Do I ever!" Angus wheeled and stuck his head through the pass-thru and yelled, "Ollie, you can come out now."

A weathered old man with rut-sized cracks in his face shuffled out from the kitchen. Long, dirty strands of hair hung like fringe from the bald place on his head.

Maxine's warning about vagrants stacking up pounded in David's head. "Who do we have here?"

"This is Ollie." Angus draped a protective arm around his friend. "He's the reason I didn't starve to death out on the road." Angus's smile lit up his eyes. "Ollie's the best cook you'll ever find, well except for my MeMaw."

"You're darn tootin'." Ruthie glowed. "However, I'm hirin' Ollie on today." Ruthie slapped her thighs. "Tell you what, David. After all you and the good folks down at Mt. Hope Community have done for me, I'll loan y'all both of these fellas to do your Christmas Eve baking." Ruthie popped the counter. "Heck, I'll even provide all the supplies."

David's head whipped from Angus to Ruthie then back to

Ollie. Anxious, hopeful smiles lit their faces. No, the light of Jesus lit their faces. Pleased laughter reverberated in David's head and he knew exactly where it came from…his father.

He had to admit something about this glorious outcome pleased him too. Immensely. More than he could have ever expected. Almost as much as it would have pleased him to have caught Amy sneaking into the diner on her lunch break.

But to turn over something as important as the Christmas Eve refreshments to these new recruits gave him a bit of heartburn. David thought about pulling Angus aside and warning him about how easily bad friends could corrupt good morals, but then he remembered his own sermon.

Time to practice the unconditional love he preached. "Then meet me at the church first thing Christmas Eve morning and we'll bake some brownies."

CHAPTER NINETEEN

"Mother, I'm perfectly capable of driving myself to the airport." Leona searched her purse for her van keys while her mother's wheelchair blocked the kitchen door.

"What if Maddie gets delayed?"

"I've checked the airline and Maddie's flight hasn't been delayed by the weather in Chicago."

"What if you're needed for some last minute Christmas Eve show prep?"

"Nellie was sweet to ask,"—Leona dug through a side pocket.—"but the girl doesn't really need me."

Roberta flicked her wrists in exasperation. "What's the use of having a chauffeur if we can't send him on a few errands?"

"I don't have a chauffeur. You do."

"Same thing."

"No, it's not, Mother."

Roberta sighed. "Melvin's been with me for years and I don't want to have to let him go, especially not right before Christmas."

Leona quit pawing through her purse. "Why would you let Melvin go?"

"I just don't need him as often anymore."

"You mean since you go everywhere in that rattletrap vehicle of the church janitor," Leona teased.

"For your information, Cotton drives a very well-maintained classic. A collector's item, really."

"Like you."

"I won't be in this wheelchair forever, Leona. Remind me to kick your backside when I get my legs under me."

"Cotton is a good man."

"It doesn't bother you that Cotton and I are...dating?"

Leona started to laugh but then she noticed her mother's embarrassment. This question was important and it deserved a serious answer. "Mother, I adored my father. But Daddy's been gone for ten years. He would have wanted you to be happy."

Roberta lifted her chin in pleased agreement. "He would have wanted me to spend every last dime."

This time, Leona couldn't contain her smile. "You've

always spent every penny Daddy made on your pleasure, and not once did I see it make Daddy anything but happy."

Her mother pushed at the back of her hair thoughtfully. "As much as I hate to admit this, Leona, I was wrong about J.D. I've watched your church friends rally around you and I've heard all the wonderful things they've said about your husband and I've learned something very important."

"Not to judge a book by its cover?"

She shrugged like she deserved the little jab, but she wasn't going to let anything deter her from finishing this conversation. "I've learned how much J.D. loved his life. At the church. In this old house. With you and the kids." Roberta took Leona's hands in hers. "Your husband may not have left you a fortune, but J.D. was a very generous man and he left you the most important thing in the world. Happiness. Don't waste his gift by grieving forever."

Tears stung Leona's eyes. "It's only been a few weeks, Mother."

"I'm not rushing you, dear." Roberta squeezed Leona's hands gently. "I'm just saying don't try to keep everything like it was. Don't be afraid to live, child. Try new things, like your job. And encourage your children to do the same."

Leona's tears were flowing so freely now, she could only nod.

"That's better." Roberta pulled a tissue from her sleeve. "We'll let Melvin pick up Maddie, and you'll let me treat us to a pedicure and a stiff drink."

Leona dabbed at her eyes. "Mother, you know I don't drink."

"You might want to start."

"What's that supposed to mean?"

"How else are we going to survive this shindig Maxine's daughter is throwing tonight?"

"You're going?" Leona couldn't contain her surprise. "You know there's a good chance they'll mention Jesus, right?"

"Cotton never misses the Christmas Eve service at Mt. Hope Community." Roberta's habit of pushing at the back of her hair cemented her decision. "And from here on out, I will never miss being with Cotton."

"Who are you, and what have you done with my mother?"

Roberta's smile was thoughtful, deep, and comforting. "I know your heart is breaking right now, my dear. But you have something I didn't."

"Faith," Leona said.

Robert gave a little nod. "That and some really good people around you."

"Why the change of heart?"

The doorbell rang.

"Oh no you don't." Roberta shook a warning finger. "I can't have you rubbing my nose in how you've been praying for me to leave the dark side." She pulled out her cell phone. "Go. Answer the door. I'm sending Melvin to the airport."

"And you think *I'm* stubborn." Leona put down her purse. "Send him. I can use the extra time to get ready for our family Christmas." She gave her mother's cheek a quick peck then ran to the front door. "Maxine—"

"I just came from the church." Maxine pushed past her, storming into the living room, then wheeling around so fast her huge handbag nearly smacked Leona in the chest. "Do you know what *your* son's done now?"

"Maxine—"

"Davy's letting *vagrants* prepare the refreshments for tonight's service."

Leona scowled, "I have no idea what you're talking about."

"There are *vagrants* in our church kitchen!" Maxine shouted.

"They're not vagrants." Roberta had rolled herself into the living room. She pushed at the back of her hair with an air of defiance. "They're caterers."

"Caterers?" Leona asked. "Mother the church can't afford caterers."

"David needed help," Roberta said. "So I suggested he

toss Cornelia's ridiculous menu and let me hire caterers to make a few treats for this little production."

"My daughter has been breaking her back to help," Maxine snarled. "She's thought through every detail, including homemade brownies in the sanctuary."

Roberta bowed up and Leona knew Maxine was fixing to get an ear full. "Your daughter has practically run everyone into the ground with rehearsals." Roberta rolled her wheelchair to within inches of Maxine. "Wilma's ankles are swollen from hours of standing behind the piano. Ivan hasn't written his newspaper column in two weeks. And poor Bette Bob's fingers are so bloody from strumming that dang guitar she couldn't stir brownie batter if her life depended upon it. If your heart wasn't a stone, you'd have hired the caterers yourself."

"Quality takes time and dedication, Roberta," Maxine defended.

"I just know Bette Bob had both the time and the energy to pop brownies in the oven when *my Leona* was running Christmas Eve," Roberta said smugly.

Maxine stepped toe to toe with Roberta's wheelchair. "Now listen here, Bertie."

"Mother. Maxine." Leona separated them, still in shock her mother not only knew so much about everyone, but actually had cared enough to step in. "Let's just all calm down and try to figure out what's going on. Start at the beginning, Maxine."

Maxine took an exasperated breath. "I stopped at the church to leave lunch for Cornelia and her band." Maxine's lifted nose implied Leona wasn't the only one who could show concern for others. "When I entered the fellowship hall, I found two strangers puttering around in the kitchen. Grinding mint. Bags of the stuff. The place will reek like a candy cane when they put those brownies in the oven."

"Strangers?" Leona asked. "Did you call David? Or the police?"

"I did not waste my time," Maxine said.

"Why not?" Leona demanded.

"Because"—Maxine rolled her eyes. –"one of the strangers was that skinny vagrant your son has taken a shine to, and when I asked the boy what he thought he was doing in *my* kitchen, he said David had not only let them in, he'd given them a key."

"First of all, it's not *your* kitchen." Leona could feel her blood beginning to boil. "And secondly, Angus is Ruthie's grandson. The boy sat behind you Sunday and he wouldn't still be a stranger to you if you'd bothered to turn around and introduce yourself."

"Well, for the record, the boy sings terribly off key."

Maxine's look radiated superiority.

"He was singing! In church!" Leona realized Maxine was trying to lead her down a path she refused to travel. "If the church won't help bring families together, who will?"

Maxine was too wound up to listen. "Well, when Ruthie sues the church after that boy empties her till, it's coming out of Davy's pay," Maxine huffed. "But I don't think even you can defend Davy allowing that *other* vagrant to have access to the church."

"What other vagrant?"

"The old codger who looked like he'd been rode hard and put up wet. We don't know him." She pointed toward the church building. "And now that stranger has a key."

"He must be a friend of Angus."

"I don't see how that makes him a friend of ours," Maxine said. "Don't you get it, Leona? David's giving strangers keys to our church building. What next? Handing out keys to our homes!"

"Angus proved to be very trustworthy while he was living here," Leona argued.

Maxine crossed her arms. "Just because a person has darkened a church door, that doesn't mean they've changed."

"Church certainly hasn't changed you one iota, Maxine." Roberta mumbled.

"Mother!"

Feathers obviously ruffled, Maxine took a big breath and plowed on, "Don't think I'm missing the significance of what David has managed to accomplish, Leona. But if we help one person, what's to keep that person from telling another person? Then another? And another? Before you know it—"

"There's a full-scale revival in this town?" Leona asked.

"Mock me all you want, Leona," Maxine said. "But I think having one vagrant sitting on our church pew last Sunday and two poking around in our church kitchen by mid-week proves what I've said before. Let one vagrant in, and the next thing you know, they're stacked up like old newspapers outside our door." Maxine's head quirked in sarcasm. "Oh, wait. They won't be stacked up outside our church building. They'll all be inside, all warm and toasty because our interim pastor gave them a key!"

"There's only one thing to do," Leona said.

"Fire the Harpers before vagrants burn our church to the ground?" Maxine huffed.

"No," Leona said as calmly as she could. "Offer to help them."

CHAPTER TWENTY

David deposited the last of Shirley's neatly folded Christmas Eve programs near the poinsettias on each side of the foyer door. The whole building had been transformed into a welcoming wonderland of red blooms and white candles. The Christmas Eve service was going to happen and he had Nell—Cornelia to thank. He couldn't believe all she'd accomplished in such a short time. He owed her a big apology for doubting both her ability to pull it off and her motivation. Not a date, just an apology.

Determined to get his thank-you over with, David strode toward the sanctuary's open doors and the beat of Ivan's drum. Cornelia had even managed to make the band sound halfway decent. Standing center stage, Cornelia lifted the mic and belted, "*In eggshells is day-a-a-a-o.*"

Her pained voice stopped David in his tracks. Struggling to breathe, Cornelia took another stab at the chorus. When she did finally manage to cough out something, she sounded more like a chain smoker than the angel her sexy, white-sequined sweater suggested.

This was not good.

Why hadn't he worked harder to convince Amy to sing? He knew why. Amy wasn't speaking to him. She'd avoided his calls, texts, and although Ruthie and Angus had denied helping Amy sneak out through the kitchen every time he came through the front door, he'd seen a flash of blonde through the pass-thru the last time he'd dropped in.

David strolled to the stage and sliced his finger across his throat to signal Cornelia to cut it off for a moment. "You okay, Nell—Cornelia?"

A pleased smile lit her face. "I'm good," she croaked as she rubbed her throat.

"Maybe you should cut your warm-up short. Save your voice for tonight."

She came to the lip of the stage and crouched down, making it difficult for David to avoid the mountainous view framed by her V-necked sweater. "We're almost there," she raised her elbow to her mouth and coughed.

"You sure you're okay?" David took a step back. "Sounds

like you may have a sore throat."

"Maybe a little." She started coughing again, so much so, David looked to the band for help. They shrugged, like they didn't know what to do but wait out their leader's hacking fit. When Nellie finally quit coughing, she began fanning her flushed face. She whispered, "Be a dear and bring me a bottle of water from the fridge in the fellowship hall."

"Sure. It's the least I can do after all you've done. It's going to be a wonderful evening for Mt. Hope Community." He smiled, genuinely. "Thanks, Nel—Cornelia."

She leaned forward and kissed his cheek. Out a show of respect he didn't wipe it off in front of her and he didn't check for braces marks, but once he was safely in the hall, he did run his sleeve over his face...in case whatever Nellie was coming down with was contagious, he told himself.

Familiar laughter, laughter he hadn't heard combined in years, floated out the fellowship hall doors. David peeked in to catch the unlikely duo in the act. Sure enough, Momma and Maxine were standing side by side around the kitchen island. They were laughing so hard, tears streamed down their faces. On the other side of the island, Angus and Ollie were entertaining them by tossing eggs back and forth.

"Hey, Momma." David came into the kitchen. "What's going on here?"

Momma swiped her eyes. "Maxine and I decided to come over and help." Her subtle message came through loud and clear. Maxine hadn't approved of his new volunteers. So why was everyone so happy, especially Maxine?

"I'm glad you're getting to know Angus and Ollie," David said.

"Davy, you've got to sample these." Maxine spoke around the big bite of brownie in her mouth. "These are the most decadent things I've ever tasted." She winked at Ollie. "I'm pretty sure it's the mint, right, Ollie?"

Ollie dumped a few green leaves in a small stone bowl. "Awe, now, Miss Maxine, you know I cain't give away my secret recipe." He began to grind the leaves to dust with a stone pestle.

"Ollie here has been telling me about all the famous folks he's cooked for." Maxine shoved the last bite of brownie in her mouth. "He once made brownies for Mick Jagger."

"No joke?" David asked.

Maxine cut herself another brownie. "Willie Nelson had Ollie on retainer until he got himself arrested."

David subtly moved the brownie platter. "Nellie, I mean Cornelia, is not going to be too pleased if you polish off all the brownies before tonight."

"These are just the samples." Maxine waved off his

concern. "Once the fresh ones come out of the oven, my Nellie won't be able to stop either," Maxine giggled. "I mean Cor-neel-ya. Doesn't seem right to call her that without Colton."

David looked at Momma who was looking at him with the same confused brow.

Maxine reached across the counter and took another brownie. "Let me tell you, Ollie, anyone who can cook like this needs to be cooking in the White House not the Koffee Kup." Maxine waved the brownie at Angus. "Everyone says you're a smart boy, Angus Freestone. I think taking up with this fine man is proof. I might have been wrong about you."

The fellowship hall door flew open. Nellie stumbled in, both hands clutched around her throat. Her mouth hung wide open in what appeared to be a silent scream.

Maxine dropped her brownie. "Nellie!"

Momma tore from the kitchen. David raced after her. They met Nellie at one of the serving tables.

"Nellie, are you choking?" Momma helped her to a chair.

Nellie shook her head. Tears streamed down her face. "It hurts," she mouthed, silently pointing at her throat. "Can't breathe."

"Maxine!" David turned. Maxine had not left the kitchen. From her horror-stricken face, he knew she was reliving the day Colton's horse went down, and her terror made him as sick then as it did now. "Maxine! Is your Caddy out back?"

Maxine could barely nod.

"Give me the keys," David shouted as he took Maxine's daughter in his arms. "We've got to get Nellie to the hospital."

CHAPTER TWENTY-ONE

The moment David and Maxine had Nellie in the car and were on their way to the hospital, Leona rushed to the sanctuary to make a plan with the band. The Christmas Eve service was less than four hours away. If the doctors at the ER couldn't give Nellie something to revive her voice, Mt. Hope's Christmas Eve service wouldn't have a singer.

Ivan laid his drum sticks on the bongo. "My Joseph robe is in storage, but I'd be happy to belt a choir robe and drape a towel over my head, Leona, if that would help."

"I appreciate the offer, Ivan," Leona chewed on her lip, mentally running a checklist of all the things that would have to happen to revive her old show. "The Moots' newborn is sick. Which means we don't have a baby Jesus."

"We had to use a doll the year the Moots didn't have a

newborn," Bette Bob offered.

Leona shook her head. "Y'all have practiced for hours. I'd hate to let your work go to waste."

"Why don't you sing, Leona?" Wilma began playing the introduction to Leona's favorite Christmas song. "Nobody can sing *Mary Did You Know* like you." She nodded her head when Leona was supposed to jump in.

"I haven't been on stage in years, Wilma." Leona sat on the front pew. "But we all know who *could* knock that song out of the park." She locked eyes with the electric guitarist.

Bette Bob shook her head. "Amy won't do it, Leona."

Leona sighed. "And it's not right to ask her."

Bette Bob undid her guitar strap. "Guess we'll have to go with a few hymns and David's reading of the Christmas story."

"And let the Episcopalians have the Christmas crowd?" Everyone turned to see who had weighed in with fighting words.

"Maddie!" Leona ran to the back of the sanctuary and wrapped her daughter in a big hug. "I'm glad you're home."

Maddie's loosened scarf revealed the chiseled good looks she'd inherited from her father. "When I landed, I had a text from David asking if I knew a magic cure for Nellie's laryngitis."

"We're hoping it's just a sore throat, maybe strained vocal

cords." Leona knew from Maddie's expression she was being overly hopeful.

After Maddie gave everyone a quick report on her residency interviews, Leona pulled her aside. "You're going to the hospital, aren't you?"

Maddie's beautiful face sobered. "Amy texted me when David brought Nellie in. She said she'd noticed a lump on Nellie's neck and tried to convince her to have it checked."

"So you're worried it could be something more serious than just a sore throat?"

"Let me go to the hospital and see what I can find out," Maddie said. "We've still got a few hours before the service."

"I'm going with you." Leona turned to Wilma and the band. "Everyone. Pray. And don't you dare pack up the band."

Leona and Maddie rushed to Mt. Hope's little hospital. They found Maxine, Howard, and David pacing the ER waiting room.

The moment Maxine saw Leona she rushed to her and buried her head in Leona's shoulder. "I can't lose another child."

Leona wrapped Maxine in a rush of forgiveness. "I'm praying you won't have to, friend." All the pent-up anger she'd had toward this woman dissolved in the puddle of their mutual tears. Bleary-eyed, Leona glanced over Maxine's shoulder.

Howard seemed equally lost. "Let's find a quiet corner." Leona led Maxine across the waiting room, got her settled in a comfy chair, then took Howard by the arm and guided him to the adjoining seat. She offered Maxine a tissue. "What can we do to help?"

"I need you to send Maddie back there."

"Maxine, I'm not certified yet," Maddie said.

"I don't care. The doc on call is that new kid who thinks we're all a bunch of illiterate goat ropers."

"Maddie?" Leona asked, her eyes pleading. "Is there anything you can do?"

"I'll offer the info Amy gave me." Maddie headed toward the swinging doors.

"You've got a good girl, Leona." Maxine dabbed at her nose. "I know I've spoiled mine," she sobbed. "Nellie's bossy and pushy. I don't know where she gets it, except that after Colton died, I just couldn't tell her no…on anything…even a band on Christmas Eve."

"Shhh." Leona wrapped her arm around Maxine. "You had to do something with all that extra love. I would have done the same thing."

"No you wouldn't have, Leona. You're a rock. A tower."

"Maxine, I'm not." Fresh tears sprang from Leona's eyes. "Since J.D. died, I've wondered how you managed to get out of bed these last ten years."

"I should have spent some of my love on you," Maxine sniffed. "Can you ever forgive me, Leona?"

"There's nothing to forgive, dear friend." They held on to each other, both painfully aware of the fragility of life and neither willing to let another precious second slip away.

Arm in arm, Leona and Maxine waited, watching the minutes tick by. Finally, Amy, Maddie, and a serious-faced doctor came out.

Leona felt Maxine tense beside her as the three of them crossed the empty waiting room to where they huddled.

"Howard. Maxine." The doctor planted his feet, a man prepared to deliver bad news. "Your daughter has a tumor on her thyroid. She's signed the permission for me to operate."

"Operate?" Maxine's breath audibly caught in her throat. "When?"

"Now."

"Is it cancer?" Howard asked.

"Cancer?" Maxine folded against Leona. "I can't lose my girl."

"Let's not borrow trouble before the labs come back, Maxine," the doctor said.

"I want Maddie to scrub in," Maxine demanded.

"That's not normal protocol."

Maxine raised up to her full five-eleven height. "There's nothing normal about my daughter."

The doctor crossed his arms. "If Nellie gives her permission, then I'll let this med student scrub in."

Relief flooded Maxine's face. "Top-of-her-class med student."

The surgeon scrunched his hat down on his brow. "Fine."

"Can I see her before surgery?" Maxine asked.

"We'll call you before we take her back." The doctor turned to Maddie. "Step it up, Harper."

David was the first to speak after the doctor and Maddie left. "Guess I'll go to the church and cancel tonight's service." Though his comment was meant for her, Leona couldn't help but notice David hadn't taken his eyes off Amy who was still hanging around the waiting room like she was waiting for a private moment to talk with him.

"Cancel?" Maxine said. "Mt. Hope Community has never cancelled a Christmas Eve service."

"Maxine, David's right," Leona said. "Our lead singer is having surgery."

"Isn't there something you can do, Leona?" Maxine asked.

"I don't know what."

Maxine clasped Leona's shoulders. "I've seen you take on a Sunday school room of toddlers with just what you happened to have in your purse."

Leona shook her head. "Ivan offered to resurrect his role as Joseph but you and I both know it's too late to round up some sheep, let alone drag the manger out of your storage barn. If we cancel now, people will have time to make other plans."

"You mean let them go to the Episcopalian Church?" Maxine strode the waiting room, her finger wagging at David. "I can't believe our interim pastor is just going to let all of my Nellie's hard work to save his bacon be for—wait one cotton-pickin' minute." Maxine stopped ranting and marched over to Amy who seemed to be trying not to let anyone catch her staring at David's distraught face. "There is one person who can keep Mt. Hope Community's Christmas Eve service from being a bust."

Amy backed up, her face suddenly pale and her palms in the air. "Maxine, I can't."

"Oh yes you can, young lady." Maxine's voice softened. "I heard you singing behind me Sunday, all soft and quiet like. For a moment I thought it was an angel, but then I remembered all those performance videos your mother used to make me watch and I realized it was you, Amy."

Amy's eyes darted between David and Maxine as she weighed her decision. "I'll do it. Just this once. For Nellie."

Maxine shook her head. "You'll do it because it's your gift."

CHAPTER TWENTY-TWO

Leona returned to the waiting room with a cup of coffee she'd purchased from a vending machine. "Drink this, Maxine."

She wrapped her shaky hands around the Styrofoam cup and gazed into the steaming contents. "You remembered."

"Three creamer packets and two Sweet'N Lows."

Maxine's eyes clouded up again. "I've missed us, Leona."

Leona sat in the empty chair between Maxine and Howard. "Me too."

"I'm going to make it up to you."

"Let's focus on Nellie for now, okay?"

Maxine nodded and raised her cup. Before she took a sip she stopped, her gaze on the open waiting room door. "Sweet boy!"

Angus shivered at the threshold, a smile on his face and a

plastic bag in his hands.

"Angus?" Leona went to him. "What are you doing here?"

"I couldn't think of anything else to do for you, so Ollie said I should bring you some brownies. Especially since Miss Maxine liked them so much."

"That's so kind of you."

He held out the bag. "Here."

"Why don't you give them to Maxine yourself?"

"I don't want to bust in where I'm not wanted."

"What's going on?" Maxine had left her seat and had come to stand beside Leona.

"Angus was worried about you." Leona passed Maxine the bag. "He brought brownies."

Maxine's face softened. "Where's your coat, sweet boy?"

Angus zipped his hoodie. "Don't have one."

"Isn't Ruthie going to buy you one?" Maxine asked.

"Soon as she can."

Maxine turned. "Howard, give the boy your coat."

Howard's head popped up. "What?"

"You heard me. Give the boy your coat."

Angus shook his head. "That ain't necessary. I'll be fine."

"It's freezing out there and I'm sure you walked here and you'll have to walk all the way back to the church. Is that right?"

Angus nodded.

"Howard has a closet full of coats and he has a nice warm car." She marched over to Howard, held out her hand until her husband gave up his leather jacket, then proudly marched back to Angus. "Button up, it's cold out there."

"Thank you." Angus slipped the coat over his hoodie.

Leona and Maxine watched the lanky kid jog out of site.

"That was amazing, Maxine."

"I can admit it when I'm wrong, Leona." She held up the bag. "Let's eat."

CHAPTER TWENTY-THREE

David rushed to the church to tell the band they were on for tonight. He couldn't believe how everything had worked out. His mother and Maxine had made up, the Harpers didn't have to move, the doctor had gotten all of Nellie's tumor, and Amy was going to sing. He could almost feel his father smiling at his newfound excitement for the mysteries of God.

"Amy must love you." Bette Bob hooked her guitar strap.

David couldn't stop the grin spreading across his face or the hope growing in his heart. "Amy loves this church."

Bette Bob peered over the neck of her guitar. "Don't let her stonewall you forever."

Uncomfortable discussing his romantic possibilities until they became reality, David changed the subject. "I promised Maxine I'd check on the refreshments." He left the band to warm up and headed for the kitchen. It was true Amy hadn't wanted Mt. Hope Community to fail on Christmas Eve, but he'd seen the way she looked at him when Maxine was twisting her arm. Amy was willing to risk her own failure to make sure he succeeded.

David pushed against the swinging door to the kitchen. "Hey, Ollie." The old guy looked up from the buttery, green mixture he was pouring into a huge bowl of chocolate batter. "Where's Angus?"

"At the hospital."

"The kid left you to do all this alone?"

"I thought that tall lady could use a hot brownie." Ollie gently stirred the batter. "Had Angus take her almost all of our first batch."

David stared at one small brownie sitting on a paper plate. "So you're telling me we don't have enough refreshments?"

"Simmer down, pastor. I doubled this new batch. Got 'em almost ready to pop in the oven. Should come out about the time the show's over."

"Service. It's called a Christmas Eve service, Ollie."

"Call it what you want, but after y'all get through entertaining everyone, me and Angus will feed 'em." Ollie lifted the last brownie from the plate. "Here, chew on this instead of me."

David let the old man drop the brownie into his palm. "Sorry, Ollie. It's just that there's a lot riding on tonight." He took a small bite. Rich chocolate melted on his tongue. "Maxine's right. These are awesome." He stuffed the whole thing in his mouth.

"Now all you need is a glass of milk." Ollie offered him a toothless grin. "Go tidy yourself up, pastor. I got your back."

David checked his watch. He didn't have time to worry about brownies. He'd have to trust this man he barely knew. He'd have to live the very words he'd preached to Amy. David scrambled for the door. If he hurried he could shower and get back in time to greet people the way his father used to do. He plowed through the back door and ran smack in to Amy. "Sorry." He reached out and steadied her. "You okay?"

She shook her head. Silent understanding passed between them. It was exactly as he'd thought. She was scared to death to sing. She'd done this for him.

"Look, Maxine shouldn't have pressured you." He couldn't stand to see her so frightened. "It's not too late to back out."

"And what am I supposed to do the next time I see Maxine?"

"Hide."

She whacked his arm. "Just because I said I would sing, that doesn't mean I can."

"Then lip sync." He pulled out his phone. "I've got Pandora on speed dial and I'm not afraid to use it." His joke rallied a fleeting smile.

Blonde strands swirled around her sober face. "What if wanting to sing isn't enough?"

"Listen to me, Amy." He pulled her to the side of the building and out of the wind. One hand holding hers, he used the other to tuck a strand of her hair behind her ear then frame her face. "You are enough if a single note never leaves that beautiful mouth of yours."

"Really?" Her lips quivered.

"More than enough. For this church. For tonight's service. For me." He noticed her gaze slide to his hold on her forearm. He wouldn't let go. Instead, he held tight until her eyes scaled slowly back to his face. Tears rimmed a faint glimmer of hope. His heart lurched. "I love you, Amy."

"But you're leaving—"

"You're not getting rid of me." David easily pulled her into his arms. Unable to stop himself, he kissed her. A kiss tethered by self-restraint so as to not scare her off, but a kiss intended to let her know he wasn't going anywhere without her. She lifted her arms around his neck and pressed her lips hard against his as if desperate to suffocate every reservation. His and hers. This time she was the one making demands, crushing the walls she'd erected.

Everything he held back flowed from his heart to hers. She alone could taste his desire, his determination to sooth her fears. He moved his hand up her back until his grip cupped her neck. Bodies entwined, she melted against him and he knew his purpose for coming home was greater than saving his mother or this church. He'd come home so this woman could save him.

When their lips finally parted, David couldn't contain his smile. "There's a Christmas band waiting for an angelic appearance."

"And there's a church waiting for their new pastor." Her fingers trailed the length of his arm searching for his hand. She linked her fingers with his, pulled him to her, and kissed him again.

Hands clasped, lips locked, they stole one more connected moment in the settling twilight. Joy flooded his soul as he watched Amy turn and smile one last time before she slipped through the door of the fellowship hall.

Adrenaline pumping, David raced home. The idea of teaming up with a feisty nurse to pastor a small town church was a thrill he'd never expected. But it was more than her kiss that had cemented the idea in his mind. It was her belief that he'd found his calling.

Taking the stairs two at a time, David yanked off his jacket and then his shirt. He was in and out of the shower in a flash. As he knotted his tie, he could feel his father's hand of approval come to rest upon his shoulder.

He strode to the closet and pulled out his father's shoes.

Tonight he would fill them and fill them well.

CHAPTER TWENTY-FOUR

The foyer was packed by the time David came rushing back to the church. Shirley wouldn't open the doors to the sanctuary until he gave her the thumbs up. David cut around back and slipped into the fellowship hall to check on the refreshment crew. Angus had returned and he and Ollie were busy starting the coffee and putting out paper dessert plates.

David sniffed, "Do y'all smell something strange?"

"A bit of batter boiled over in the oven." Ollie fanned the red and green napkins better than David had ever seen his mother do for one of her fancy showers.

"Sure stinks." David sniffed again. "Smells more like a skunk." David sniffed again trying to identify the source of the odor.

"Maybe you're just paranoid." Angus sprinkled salt over the

fresh coffee grounds in the basket filter. "Like you said, lots riding on this night. If we're going to be salt, we need to put our best foot forward." He held up the coffee basket. "That's why I'm breakin' out my secret recipe."

"You catch on quick, kid." David dug a long-tip lighter from one of the kitchen drawers. "I'll have an exterminator come after Christmas to make sure we don't have a furry family living under the building." David thanked Ollie and Angus again then hurried to the sanctuary.

After flipping the sound system to play pre-recorded Christmas carols until the service began, David stuck his head into the baptistry changing room to wish Amy and the band good luck. Wilma, Bette Bob, and Ivan were huddled around Amy and praying. Knowing his well-wishes couldn't top the power from above, David backed out quietly. He couldn't contain the smile on his face, the one his mother would recognize immediately as love. He didn't care if the whole world thought he should still be mourning his father's death, it was God who'd brought so much good out of bad and he was going to celebrate. Both during the worship service and after. He and Amy had a lot of kissing and planning to do.

David flicked the lighter. He hoped lighting the candles Momma and Nellie had placed around the sanctuary would eliminate the strange smell permeating the building. Once he had the stage lights set, he dimmed the house lights and stared at the twinkling effect of Nellie and his mother's combined work.

Beautiful.

Maybe even the most beautiful holiday presentation Mt. Hope Community had ever offered its visitors. He jogged to the closed sanctuary doors and tapped out the signal alerting Shirley they were ready for business.

As usual, the Story twins were the first through the door.

"David." Nola Gay Story tugged his suit jacket. "A little something for your family." Nola held out a mason jar filled with her famous candied cucumbers and topped with a faded sticky green bow, the same gift they gave the Harpers every year.

"Thanks, Nola Gay," David said, admiring the dark red spears. "My favorite."

Nola's twin, Etta May, stepped forward. "Sister and I know this first Christmas without your daddy will be hard." She slipped him an envelope sealed with several pieces of scotch tape. "Do something nice for your momma."

From the bulk of the envelope, David suspected it was filled with a wad of at least fifty ones, money that had probably taken them a year to save. "I can't take this, Etta May."

"It's ten percent of our windfall." Etta May pushed the

envelope back at him. "Cotton gave us a little tip that yielded more than our cucumbers ever have."

"Then you should give it to the Lord."

"Oh, we've put another fat check in the plate." Nola Gay beamed. "This is for you and your family."

"You girls are the best." David slid the envelope into his jacket pocket and tucked the jar of pickles under his arm. "No wonder my father had a crush on you."

The sisters blushed and giggled.

Nola Gay's brow furrowed. "Smells like we have skunks."

"Could be," David admitted with a resigned sigh. "Wish they hadn't picked tonight to make their presence known."

"Parker will know what to do," Etta May said before she and Nola Gay toddled off to their regular pew.

Of course, the county extension agent would know how to handle a varmint invasion. Maybe he should have Parker check it out before the service started. Wouldn't want anything to spoil tonight.

David worked his way through the crowd while texting his old friend Parker.

Be there in 5. Parker texted back.

David put his phone away and decided to not worry about the skunks for now and enjoy the fruits of his labors. As members introduced him to the friends and neighbors they'd proudly brought with them, the thrill at how many had taken his Sunday sermon seriously put a bounce in his step.

"Grandmother!" David leaned down and kissed the glowing woman seated in the wheelchair Cotton pushed. "I'm shocked."

"You know how I hate to miss a good show," his grandmother smiled.

Cotton clapped David on the shoulder and winked. "God works in mysterious ways, boy."

"That he does, Cotton. That he does."

"David."

He turned to see his sister standing with open arms. "Maddie!" He scooped her up and twirled her around. He set her down and clasped her shoulders. "Does this mean Nellie's going to be alright?"

"She came through surgery fine. Waiting on labs." Maddie tilted her head toward the door where Momma and Maxine stood, their arms draped around each other's shoulders. "The minute she came to, Nellie insisted I bring them to the church."

"She's wanting a full report on her stand-in."

Maddie pulled David aside. "I think we have a bigger problem than Nellie's jealousy over Amy."

His brow furrowed in confusion. "What now?"

Maddie jerked her head toward the door and whispered, "They're both high."

"Momma and Maxine?" David laughed. "That's crazy."

"Their eyes are bloodshot."

He shrugged. "They've been crying all afternoon."

"Their reaction times are delayed."

He watched his mother and Maxine stagger to the bench. "They're old."

Maggie bowed up, put out he was making her jump through technical hoops rather than take her trained medical opinion as fact. "They're starving," she growled between clenched teeth.

"They probably haven't had dinner."

"David, they ate a whole plate of brownies in the hospital waiting room and Maxine demanded I stop at the corner gas station for chips."

He glanced at the bench. Momma was seated with her head leaning against the wall. A mellow grin pleated her face as she watched Maxine, who was draped in fur and as animated as a cartoon character in fast-forward mode.

"Why is Maxine talking so fast and dancing around?"

"I told you, they're high."

"Why did you let them get high?" David whispered.

"Don't you know weed when you smell it?" Maddie inhaled

deeply. "Somebody is cooking pot."

Suddenly the familiarity of the odor he'd blamed on skunks smacked him between the eyes. He'd been so preoccupied by all the details he'd totally pushed his memories of frat house parties from his mind. What an idiot. "Ollie's brownies!" Terror griped David's chest. "I gotta get back there."

The sound of Ivan's drum rumbled in the sanctuary. "Too late," Maddie said. "Don't you have to do the welcome?"

David rubbed his temples, trying to think. He pointed at Momma and Maxine. "Put those two on the back row and don't let them move." He thrust the Storys' pickles at Maddie. "After I do the welcome, I'll try to slip out and shut down our marijuana edibles production line before someone calls the cops."

"Who's smokin' weed?" Parker stuck his head inside Maddie and David's huddle and pointed at Momma and Maxine. "Are those two high?"

"Shhh!" David and Maddie said simultaneously.

"Nobody's smoking, Parker." Maddie tilted her head toward Momma and Maxine. "They've accidentally ingested an unknown substance."

"Whatever they ate, it's nailing them harder than a hit from a bong," Parker said.

David and Maddie stared at Parker in shocked disbelief.

Parker shrugged off their speechlessness. "Ingested weed gets metabolized by the liver, so technically the delta-9 TCH becomes 11-hydroxy-TCH which passes the blood barrier more rapidly and leads to a heightened psychedelic effect. Those two are in for one heck of a ride."

"Who are you?" Maddie asked Parker with a mixture of frustration and pure admiration.

"Plant Biology 101," Parker smiled, pleased he'd finally gotten Maddie's attention. "They'll be stoned for four to eight hours." He sniffed the air. "Smells like we're all going to feel pretty good before this night is over." He gave David's shoulder a playful punch. "At least you know you don't have skunks."

From the sanctuary came the sound of Ivan impatiently brushing the cymbals again, this time more urgently.

"Parker, stop spouting science and make yourself useful," Maddie ordered. "Peel Momma off the bench while I try to rope in Maxine."

"Patience, grasshopper." Parker winked at Maddie.

"Parker!" David whispered. "This isn't funny, man."

"David, go!" Maddie pushed him toward the sanctuary doors.

David bolted down the aisle. He could tell the house was packed long before he took the stage in one leap. The thrill of actually pulling Christmas off temporarily had been flushed from his mind. He flicked on the mic and threw himself into a welcome he hoped sounded heartfelt and warm. As he finished up, his peripheral vision caught the slight swaying of Amy as she waited in the shadows. She was pale and struggling to breathe in and out. If the pot fumes were getting to her, no telling what would happen when she tried to sing. "And now, we'll be blessed by the songs of Amy Maxwell."

He walked over to Amy and gave her his hand-held mic. Her fingers were cold as they brushed his. "You okay?" he whispered.

"I've got a headache," she mouthed back. "Sit on the front row, please."

He mentally stuttered between saving his own neck and saving Amy. "You got it, beautiful." He winked and squeezed her free hand. "Remember, you're enough."

Amy took her place on the stage. And David took his place on the front row. The spotlights came up slowly, framing her terrified face in a hazy glow. David looked up. Pot smoke swirled from the air ducts pointed at the stage.

Wilma plucked out the intro bars on the electric keyboard.

Amy closed her eyes and opened her mouth but nothing came out. Her eyes flew open and frantically searched the front row for David.

He gave her a short nod, meant for only her. Silent encouragement passed between them. Amy took a steadying breath, but David held his. Wilma began the intro one more time. Amy closed her eyes. David watched the smoke drift down toward the stage. Amy's first notes were shaky but they were right on pitch. She smiled and took a relieved breath. By the time she reached the part where the narrator asks Mary about her baby boy walking on water, it was as if angels had hijacked Amy's nerves and filled her lungs with pure stardust. Or pot smoke? David wasn't sure which and he didn't care. She was singing. Not just for him, but for her.

As Amy's voice climbed to the crescendo, warmth flushed through David. He was helplessly in love and completely unaware that the sickly sweet smell wafting over the stage had now spread throughout the sanctuary.

Amy lowered her mic to thunderous applause. She beamed at David, who was clapping loudest of all. Once everyone had quieted but before Ivan could move on to the next number, Maxine twirled down the aisle, shouting, "I feel like I'm in one of those god-awful music videos." She spun toward the stage.

David lunged for the whirl of fur. "Maxine." The hem of the elder's wife's coat knocked him off balance as she twirled out of reach. David stumbled, empty-handed to the other side of the stage.

Maxine did a wobbly pirouette up the center steps. "How could Mary have known what would happen to her son? What mother ever does?" She ripped the mic from Amy's hands and plastered her own lips to the head. She turned and faced the audience. "I told Howard if he bought that damn horse I'd never sleep with him again."

"Maxine!" Howard's voice boomed from the back of the sanctuary. "What in the name of all that's holy are you doing?"

His wife wavered back and forth, her hand rising slowly to shield her eyes from the spot. She squinted until she located her husband. "I'm telling these people the truth, Howard."

David heard Momma scream, "Maxine, don't."

Momma, Maddie, and Parker ran down the aisle. By the time they reached the stage, Maxine had crumpled in uncontrollable sobs.

"It's Howard's fault." Maxine cried into the mic. "He killed my boy."

Horrified chatter rippled across the auditorium.

Nola Gay stood up and faced the crowd. "Nothing to see here folks. Let's escape this foul smell and adjourn to the fellowship hall for some brownies."

"No!" David grabbed the microphone and announced, "No one eat the brownies!"

Maxine babbled nonsensically throughout David's brief explanation and apology. She cranked it up to wailing while the sanctuary emptied at a snail's pace. No one was willing to admit it, but everyone was dying to know what else the elder's wife would scream at her husband, even though Howard was long gone, having been the first one out the front door.

David did not drop on the front pew until Parker had cleared everyone but Maddie, Amy, Momma, Maxine, and the sickly sweet smell of chocolaty pot. David looked at his shoes. His feet were killing him. If he could kick off his father's shoes here and now, he'd throw them across the sanctuary and never put them on again.

"Anything else I can do?" Parker asked Maddie who was crouched beside Maxine and trying to get her to be still long enough to examine her.

"Her vitals are good and she's not having any chest pain." Maddie told him. "I think she just needs to sleep it off."

"Want me to take her home?" Parker asked.

Maddie looked around. "Guess you'll have to. I don't think Howard's coming back any time soon. David and I can get Momma home."

Momma's red-heeled feet hung over the edge of the pew where she'd passed out.

David felt a firm hand on his shoulder. He glanced behind

him.

Saul Levy. Great.

"I'll help your sister escort your mother home while you deal with the situation in the kitchen." Saul hadn't threatened. He didn't have to. David knew Mt. Hope Community wasn't legally out of the woods. Etta May's promise to activate the prayer chain had set the local police sirens in motion.

"Thanks, Mr. Levy."

As David pushed himself up from the pew his grandmother wheeled up, a pleased smile lighting her face. "Now that's what I call a Christmas Eve show."

CHAPTER TWENTY-FIVE

Snowflakes swirled in the freezing wind as Amy followed David to the car. "I'm coming with you." She hopped into the passenger seat of Leona's van and shut the door before he could argue.

David got in and pumped the gas. "It could be a long night."

"Don't think you're getting rid of me that easy," she teased as she reached across the console and squeezed his hand. "I got you into this mess. Only right I help get you out."

"I would do it again, you know?" In the light of the dash, she saw a flicker of the smile her kisses had put on his face earlier. "In all the craziness"—his breath puffed out in little white clouds—"I didn't get a chance to tell you how amazing you are." He drew their clasped hands to his lips and kissed hers. "Adele better watch her back."

Warmth surged through Amy's limbs. "And you better see where they're taking our boy."

They followed the flashing blue lights of the police cruiser to the station. Angus climbed out of the back of the squad car, his hands cuffed. The van's headlights shone on his terrified face.

Amy and David jumped out and ran to him.

"Don't say anything, Angus," David shouted over the wind.

"Angus!" Ruthie rushed up. "I'm here, boy."

"I'm sorry, MeMaw." Angus ducked his head in shame. "I wasn't thinkin'." He let the officer lead him inside.

"Help my boy, David." Ruthie begged. "He didn't know."

Ollie had slipped out the back door of the fellowship hall long before the sirens arrived. While Amy was sure the old man had tried to take Angus with him, the boy had stayed behind to comfort Ruthie. What Ruthie was saying was probably true. Angus had no idea Ollie was cooking marijuana edibles. Convincing a judge would take some doing. Convincing Maxine, once she came down off her high, would take a miracle.

By the time Amy and David put Ruthie and Angus in her car after taking care of all the bail formalities, pink streaks cut through dark gray clouds. Skiffs of snow dusted the awnings of several downtown buildings.

Hand in hand Amy and David walked to the van. He reached for the door handle, but before he could help her inside she pulled him to her. "Merry Christmas, David."

"Not exactly how I planned our first Christmas together."

She put her hands on his cold cheeks and drew his lips close to hers. "Wait until you see what kind of mess I get you into next year."

"Bring it on, woman."

Their kiss was a mixture of relief and worry. They both knew the crisis had not been averted, only diverted. The real impact of what had happened had yet to reverberate through the church and when it did, more than stained-glassed windows would shake. Heads were likely to roll. Theirs.

For now, none of that mattered. Amy pressed deeper, drinking in the feeling of being safely wrapped in the arms of a man not afraid to take on a challenge. Her included.

For now, it was Christmas morning and God had given her the greatest gift of all. Unconditional love.

CHAPTER TWENTY-SIX

Momma was exceptionally quiet when she finally emerged from her bedroom somewhere around three Christmas afternoon. David wasn't sure if her melancholy was the result of the aftermath of her first high or the mess they'd made of their first Christmas without Dad.

If either of them had been in a better mood, they might have appreciated the Christmas miracle of Maddie and Grandmother working together to put a meal on the table. A meal none of them had the heart to eat.

He needed to know what to do. "Momma?"

She raised her palm. "We'll talk tomorrow."

The day after Christmas Momma didn't come down to breakfast. Turmoil rumbled in David's gut. He'd burst if he sat around and did nothing another day.

He should right the situation on his own. After all this wasn't Momma's mess. It was his.

He'd start by airing out the church.

David donned an old sweatshirt and headed across the parking lot. He opened the door to the fellowship hall. The place still reeked. He cringed at his foolishness and started propping doors open. Holding his breath, he jogged through the building and jammed the door stops under the sanctuary doors in hopes of creating a cross-draft.

Now for the mess in the kitchen. It took him an hour to shove uneaten brownies down the disposal, bag the crusty mixing bowls, and haul anything pot had touched to the dumpster. For good measure, he bleached every kitchen surface and wiped out the oven. His teeth chattering from the cold wind whipping through the building, he sniffed. The skunky smell remained. It had even infiltrated his father's office.

He'd just wedged an old paint stick under the window sash behind his father's desk when the door suddenly flew open.

"Here you are, you coward." Maxine stood with hands on hips, her nostrils flaring.

David wiped his numb fingers on his sweatshirt. "I was waiting until after the holidays to talk to you, Maxine."

"After the holidays or after I sobered up?"

"I'm sorry—"

"Did I or did I not warn you about taking in vagrants?"

Maxine's fiery breath blasted him in front. "You were right." Cold air blasted him in the back. "I admit it."

"Not only are the Episcopalians having a good laugh at the expense of Mt. Hope Community, the entire town is laughing at me." She stormed to his desk, her red-rimmed eyes flashing. "Howard hasn't spoken to me in two days."

"I'm sorry, Maxine."

"Don't blame the Harpers," Maxine snarled as she snugged her fur coat closed. "That's what Howard has preached at me for years. And then, when I finally do what he says, less than two hours later I'm drugged by one of the Harper vagrants."

"Look, I know Christmas Eve was a bust—"

"Bust?" Maxine screeched. "It was a catastrophe of Biblical proportions!"

"In the future, I'll be more careful," David promised through chattering teeth. "Supervise our converts more closely."

"Future?" Maxine's finger tapped the desk. "There is no future for you here, Davy."

"But—"

"I've got the Board on my side." She waved her hand. "You're lucky I talked them out of suing."

"For what?"

"For ruining the reputation of Mt. Hope Community Church!"

"You mean your reputation."

Maxine shuddered. "You've got twenty-four hours to pack up your belongings and go." She wheeled and crashed into Momma who was standing behind her with her mouth hanging open in silent disbelief. "And take your mother with you." Maxine shouted as she pushed past Momma.

David smacked his palm against his father's shelf of commentaries. "That is one mean woman."

Momma came in. "She's hurting, David."

"Enough with the excuses," David shouted. "I'm sick of you covering for her."

"She's my friend."

"She's not."

Momma pointed behind him. "Mind closing the window."

"You think God's going to open a door? He's not."

"David, you didn't fail here."

"Are you still high?"

Momma rubbed her temples. "Maybe a little hung over, but definitely back to reality."

"I failed you." David spun and fisted the paint stick free from the window sash. The window slammed shut with a jarring rattle. "You warned me about trying to save the underdogs." He dropped into his father's chair.

Momma reached for the Bible that was on the corner of the desk. "I want to show you something."

"Don't preach at me, Momma."

"It's not preaching if it's the Lord speaking." She flipped the onion-skinned pages until she found the passage she was searching for. "Colossians 1:9-10." She slid the Bible across the desk. "Read it."

David blew out an exasperated sigh and snatched up the Bible. His father had underlined the verse in red ink. "So?" He pushed it back at her.

"So, doing kind things for others is what pleases the Lord." Momma sat in the chair on the opposite side of the desk. "And that, James David, is never a fail."

"Momma, don't you get it? All is lost." David raked his hair. "Ollie left town before I could offer to represent him. Ruthie believes since she failed to raise her daughter, she'll fail at raising Angus." David had never felt so hopelessly cold and red-hot mad at the same time. "We lost, Momma. We have to move."

"David, I'd live under the overpass myself if it would make things better between Maxine and Howard. They've got to work this out. And they will. They love each other." Momma leaned forward. "My advice to you was wrong. Getting mixed up with Angus is exactly what your father would have done."

"Obviously he knew how to clean up his messes, because he lasted eighteen years."

"Your father lasted until his work here was done."

"This is as good as it gets?"

Momma shrugged. "Cornelia is going to live. On the positive side, you won't have to avoid dark baptistry rooms for the rest of your life."

"I love you, Momma."

"And I have never been prouder of you, son."

"What am I going to tell Amy?" David asked. "We were planning a life here."

"I think you don't need my advice on this one." Momma stood. "Oh, I almost forgot why I popped over. I promised Saul we'd settle J.D.'s estate after Christmas. I made an appointment. He's expecting us in thirty minutes."

Another punch landed in David's gut. "Let me close up." He stood and let his gaze take in the serenity of his father's office one last time. "Wouldn't want vagrants to get in."

CHAPTER TWENTY-SEVEN

Leona eased the van into the last parking space in front of Dewey Hardware. Hands gripping the wheel, she let the engine idle. The heater never had warmed up and her feet were frozen. She'd sounded brave for her children's sake, but her insides coiled in fear. She loved this town. She loved Mt. Hope Community Church. And she loved the house she'd lived in the past eighteen years. She'd made the parsonage into a home. Leaving everything she knew terrified her.

"Momma?" Maddie's hand touched her shoulder. "Ready?"

Leona glanced at Maddie's supportive face in the rearview mirror. "Sure." She let her gaze slide to her stoic son riding shotgun. "A change could do us all some good. Right, David?"

"Hope you're right," he sighed. "'Cause it doesn't look like we have a choice."

Together, the Harper family climbed the steps to the lawyer's office. Juanita, the secretary Saul had inherited when he bought the firm, led them to the conference room. "Anyone need coffee?" she asked.

"We're good, Juanita. Thanks," Leona said.

David pulled out a chair. "Here, Momma."

Leona sat facing the windows, her forearms resting on the table for support. David and Maddie flanked her on either side. Leona reached out and took each of their hands.

Two minutes later, Saul came in, a thick file resting in the crook of his elbow. "Things back to normal at the church?"

Leona felt David stiffen. "Pretty much."

Saul dropped the file on the table. "The judge tells me that because Ollie left a note saying the pot was his, proving Angus had no knowledge of his … activities … David was able to get the boy off with a light sentence of community service." Saul took his place at the head of the table. "I guess all is forgiven then?"

"Except by Maxine," Leona said. "The Board is voting this evening."

"On what?" Saul asked.

"On whether the Harpers go or stay." David's terse tone told Leona he was taking this harder than she would have expected.

"It should be an easy decision then."

"Maxine has already secured the support she needs to have us removed," Leona said.

Saul's face sobered. "That's a shame."

"Don't worry about us," David said. "We'll be fine."

"Oh, I have no doubt of that." Saul clasped his hands over the file. A rare look of compassion came over his face. "It's just that I hate to think of Mt. Hope losing such a fine family."

Leona tried to swallow the terror creeping up her throat. "Thank you, Saul."

"Is there anything I can do?"

"No," Leona said firmly. "But thanks."

"Not only have you and J.D. blessed my life, Leona"—Saul turned his attention to David—"I believe your son has a gift for the pulpit and I would hate to see that gift wasted."

"That's kind of you, Saul," Leona whispered, fighting tears at the actual reality sinking in. She was moving. After eighteen years, she was leaving the community she'd come to love and she thought loved her. "The Lord never wastes anything we give him with our whole heart."

"Can we wrap this up?" David asked. "We've got a lot of packing to do and I've got to rent a U-Haul before they close."

"You can afford professional packers if you want." Saul tapped the file. "Or you can even afford to buy the parsonage if you'd rather not move."

"What are you talking about?" David asked.

"I believe you can make the church a handsome offer if you want to keep your house, Leona. An offer even Maxine Davis could not refuse."

"I couldn't put a down payment on a pup tent, Saul." Leona said. "What makes you think I could possibly buy the parsonage?"

"This." Saul opened the file and handed her a piece of paper edged in a beautiful scroll. A certificate of stock ownership. "You are a very wealthy woman, Leona."

Leona's heart stopped. She didn't blink. She didn't move. It was as if someone had shoved her head under water and she couldn't breathe.

"What did you say?" David's garbled question was the very one she would have asked if she could speak.

"The TauRx shares J.D. left you are worth millions. Fifteen million to be exact."

Leona came up for air and sputtered, "I don't understand."

"J.D. invested a small monthly amount in this particular pharmaceutical stock." Saul handed her a piece of paper with so many dollar signs and zeros her eyes blurred. "Pennies on the dollar, really."

Maddie assumed a wary posture. "How would Dad even

know about this company?"

"Cotton." Leona's mind retraced all the times she'd caught the church janitor and J.D. huddled together. Once she'd even seen them looking at a file, a file Cotton had said contained notes to a Bible study he was considering. She intended to track Cotton down at the church. Whether she'd hug him or kick him for helping J.D. keep her in the dark she didn't know. "Cotton's rich too, isn't he?"

Saul gave her the same don't-go-there look David had given her at the diner. "I'm not at liberty to discuss the financial affairs of your very wise, retired-banker friend."

"And all this time Mother thought falling in love with Cotton meant she'd finally learned to be self-sacrificing." Leona busted out laughing. "The woman can't lose, can she? Everything she touches turns to gold."

"Including men," David said.

"The same can be said of you, Leona." Saul passed more stacks of paper around the table. "Should this promising new Alzheimer drug pass FDA approval, your wealth could more than double overnight."

Leona and the kids flipped through the papers. When she got to the bottom line, she grabbed the hands of her children to keep from sliding from her seat. "We can go anywhere we want."

Maddie squeezed her back. "I'd loved the hospital in New York, but didn't think I could ever afford to live there."

Leona smiled. "Baby, we can afford for you to do your residency on the moon if that's what you want." She turned to David. "Where do you want to go? Back to England? Another degree from Harvard? Name it."

David pulled his hand away. "I don't know, Momma."

CHAPTER TWENTY-EIGHT

David sat on the front pew in the quiet sanctuary, his father's shoes dangling from his crooked fingers. He stared up at the empty pulpit framed in the sunlight streaming through the stained glass window. He'd fought his love-hate relationship with this huge hunk of carved wood for as long as he could remember. Why couldn't he shake the hold this pulpit had on him? Especially now that God had just dumped a truck-load of manna. So much money that he would never have to work again, let alone preach for a dying West Texas church in order to keep a roof over his mother's head. And yet, here he was, unable to walk away. Why?

"Leona said I'd find you here." Amy's hand caressed the back of his neck.

David dropped his father's shoes and gave her a weary

smile over his shoulder. "I didn't hear you come in."

She came around the pew and sat beside him. "Deep in prayer?"

"Deep in battle."

Her brow knit in confusion. "You won."

"It's crazy, I know, but it doesn't feel like a victory."

"The Board voted to keep you."

"How crazy is that? Especially after the Christmas Eve fiasco."

"I guess Hank and Harold aren't the puppets Maxine believed them to be after all."

"That, and I'm pretty sure Howard is still mad at Maxine," David added.

"You think Howard voted to have you ordained as the permanent pastor to get even with his wife?"

David shrugged. "Like you said, grief-based anger isn't always rational."

Amy leaned forward and took him by the chin. "So I'm guessing this long face, the handsome one I want to kiss by the way, isn't about how the Board voted?"

He sighed. "I'm not sure how I'm going to vote."

"I don't understand," she said. "Your family can afford to go anywhere."

David's head whipped around. "You're the only one I've

told about the money."

Amy dragged her fingers across her lips like she was closing a zipper. "The Harper secret is safe with me."

"Momma deserves a little time to process all of this. She doesn't want anyone to know she's rich. She says they'll treat her different once they find out."

"So she's staying?"

"I don't know."

"She could buy the parsonage."

"She could buy this church and this whole town, if that's what she wants," David said. "I don't know what she'll do."

"Will she at least buy a new van?"

David gave her a half-hearted chuckle. "Not until the engine falls out of that one."

"David, look at me." Amy took his hand. "Don't stay because of me."

"We've been through all that," David said, the possibility of losing her snapping him from his distraction. "I love you."

"I think you love the *idea* of you and me changing this church."

"What's that supposed to mean?"

"When you thought you were trapped in this one-stoplight-town …" her voice trailed off.

"You think I fell in love with you because I didn't have

another option?"

"I'm just saying … I want you to be sure."

David cupped her face with his hands. "The girl I fell in love with is smart. Tenacious. Honest. And kind. She loves salads and sweet tea and anyone who's been kicked to the curb." He wiped the tears from her cheek with his thumb. "Whatever God has in store for you, he has in store for me, Amy."

"David, if you stay to preach, you can't do it for me, and"—she pointed at his father's shoes—"and you can't do it for him."

He kissed the tip of her nose. "I know." He dropped his elbows to his knees and rested his head in his hands. Amy did the same.

Side by side, they sat silently, each contemplating the weight of what was at stake. The baptistry heater kicked on. David's eyes lifted to the stained glass window and the crucifixion scene that had always fascinated him. The jeweled path started wide at the base, curved around, and disappeared into a tiny point beneath a large cross.

For as long as he could remember, the fear of losing himself had kept him away from this path, the path his father had taken.

David closed his eyes. As he sucked in a labored breath, a

small voice whispered that he should look at the scene again. His eyes flew open and his gaze immediately cut to Amy. She was silent, staring straight ahead, like she hadn't heard or said anything. The instruction to look at the cross had not come from her.

David blinked and dared to look at the scene again. Radiant spears of light burst from the center of the cross and cut straight through him with an illuminating power. This cross that he'd avoided most of his life did not represent persecution but resurrection.

And now, the shafts of light were reaching well past him. They were piercing the darkness of the world. "Salt and light," a soft voice whispered. It wasn't a demand from above but rather a gentle whisper from his heart. A whisper he could trust.

Realization, bright as the sun shining through the window, dawned. His days of running in purposeless circles were over.

David picked up his father's shoes. Without a word of explanation to Amy, he carried them up the steps of the stage and to the podium. He squatted behind the pulpit and peered inside the cavity. The little stepstool waited in the dark. He gently placed his offering of worn-out shoes atop the leg-up his father had built for him. His father's influence was the bedrock upon which he would always stand. A legacy he would deny no longer. But the calling, the voice beckoning him to step out in faith, was his own.

"Well done, good and faithful servant," he whispered to the retired footwear. Covered in peace, he rose confidentially. "It's time I stood on my own two feet." He strode boldly to the lip of the stage.

Light from the stained glass had shifted. Golden rays framed an angel waiting in the aisle. David smiled at the beautiful woman smiling at him and dropped to one knee. "Amy Maxwell will you marry this imperfect, blundering, stubborn preacher man?"

"I let you go once." A coy expression danced in her eyes. "But then a handsome young pastor told me I am the kind of girl who never makes the same mistake twice."

He opened his arms and she ran to him.

EPILOGUE

Late Summer of the Following Year

To the thunderous cheers of a packed sanctuary, Leona blinked away tears as Mr. and Mrs. David Harper danced down the aisle. The wooden pews and stained glass windows of Mt. Hope Community Church had made for a beautiful afternoon wedding. Her son was happy. The members were excited about the church's future with David and Amy at the helm. And, more than once, she'd seen Maddie glance favorably in Parker's direction during the wedding. All in all, it had been a wonderful day.

So why the tears?

Leona's bleary gaze traveled back to the stage. The pastor waiting to deliver the formal reception invitation was not her J.D. Her husband would have loved sharing this day with their family. It had been nearly a year since his death, but time had not lessened her pain. In fact, with each passing moment the ache in her heart seemed to increase. But she refused to let her overwhelming loneliness ruin David's day. A day she'd prayed for since the moment her son was born. A day she prayed would come to Maddie when she was ready.

After the post-ceremony pictures were finally finished, Leona went to the foyer to give herself a stern talking to before facing a jovial crowd at the reception. She burst through the swinging doors and plowed smack into her husband's lawyer.

"Sorry, Saul."

"Leona." He held her by the shoulders. "Are you all right?" Dressed in a summer linen suit, he didn't appear as stern as he had whenever the business of settling J.D.'s affairs summoned her to his office.

She nodded. "A little emotional is all."

"Weddings are hard."

"David will be glad you came."

He released her, but his eyes continued to cut straight through her. "Let's not fool ourselves."

Saul was right. He'd grated on her son like nails on a chalkboard from their first meeting. When she'd brought his name up to David, it was quite obvious her son's opinion of his father's lawyer hadn't changed. Truth be known, she had her own reasons for not trusting the man. He'd kept J.D.'s secret from her for years. Miffed as she was at her husband's lawyer, leaving him off the guest list would have seemed an intentional slight, a slight she couldn't afford to make until she could figure out a way around J.D.'s little clause that Saul remain her financial and legal advisor.

"Then I'm glad you came." Which she hoped sounded convincing. "You are coming to the reception, aren't you?"

"Yes." He started toward the door, then turned. "May I offer you a ride?"

"Mother insists on having Melvin chauffer the family to the country club." She hadn't meant to sound so excluding. "But save me a dance."

"I don't dance."

"Oh," Leona stuttered.

"But I do eat cake." The slight twitch beneath his moustache was almost reminiscent of a smile.

If she didn't know better, she could've sworn Saul had just taken a stab at a joke. A poor one, but an uncharacteristic stab nevertheless. "Then I'll see you at the dessert table. Bette Bob has outdone herself."

She was watching Saul march from the church, contemplating why his relationship with her husband grated on her as well, when Maddie's arm slid through hers.

"David invited Daddy's attorney?" Maddie asked.

"I did."

Maddie smiled and sighed, "He *is* handsome, in a Tom-Selleck-sort-of-way."

Leona corralled her turbulent emotions before looking at her daughter. The brilliant brain residing beneath those cascading curls would pick up on her low spirits in a heartbeat. "I shouldn't have let you watch Quigley Down Under so many times with your father."

"You can't mope around forever, you know."

"I'm not moping."

"I miss Daddy, too." Maddie tugged her close and kissed her cheek. "Family days like this are especially hard."

Leona nodded. "Your father couldn't wait to walk you down the aisle."

"See, your well-meaning prying is the very reason I must distract you with your own love life," Maddie said, unthreading her arm. "I'm not going to marry."

Maddie had made this claim when Leona went to New York to get her settled for residency. Leona prayed time and the distance from the family would bring about a loneliness that would change her mind.

"I understand that giving a serious relationship the energy it deserves would be difficult while you're pursuing your dreams." Leona could tell from Maddie's expression she was fighting a losing battle, but for Maddie's own good, she had to try. "After you've finished your residency, and your life slows down, I suspect you'll want a family then."

"Life isn't going to slow down for me, Momma. Besides, I'm counting on David and Amy to drown you in so many grandchildren that I won't ever have to jump in."

For a moment, Leona considered sharing what she knew about Amy's condition, but Parker walked up and saved her from breaking David's confidence. "You look so handsome in that tux, Parker." She elbowed Maddie. "Doesn't he, Maddie?"

"He cleans up okay," Maddie said with a begrudging smile.

"Feel kind of like a stuffed sausage." Parker tugged at his collar. "How's New York, Maddie?"

"I love it," Maddie said. "Lots to do."

"Good thing you've got four years to get it all done."

"Longer if I do a fellowship."

The flash of disappointment in Parker's eyes led to an awkward pause. Maddie and Parker had been like brother and sister since middle school. Poking, teasing, they never let the other get by with anything. Not once had either of them ever been at a loss for words…at least they hadn't until they went off to different colleges and their lives took different paths. Parker loved small towns. Maddie wanted a life in the city.

Parker was laid back and low-keyed. Maddie was high strung and adrenaline driven. They knew this about each other. Accepted their relationship for the friendship it was.

So why was Leona feeling the need to say something, anything, to bridge the growing gap? Because she didn't want her daughter to end up as lonely as she was, that's why.

Leona pointed to the tiny scar last year's icy interstate spin-out had left above the young man's eye. "How's your head, Parker?"

He caressed the thin, white line like it was a tender badge of honor. "Thanks to Dr. Harper here, I still have half a brain." He hooked his finger in the knot in his tie and pulled it loose with a sigh of relief. "When do you head back, Maddie?"

"Tomorrow."

"Trust me to drive you to the airport?"

Maddie hesitated, and in that split second of uncertainty, Leona saw hope.

"You can start by driving her to the reception," Leona suggested, far too abruptly for the suggestion to be considered subtle.

Maddie's face clouded. "I thought the family was supposed to ride in Grandmother's limo."

"Melvin's not brought the car around." Leona pushed her daughter toward Parker. "She won't mind if you go on ahead."

"I'll ride with Parker, if you'll ride with Saul," Maddie challenged.

"I'm afraid Mr. Levy has already left," Leona argued.

"Nope." Parker pointed at the man getting into a Lexus on the far side of the parking lot. "Want me to flag him down?"

"She does." Maddie grabbed her mother's hand and whispered, "If I can't spend the rest of my life alone, then neither can you."

Dying to know if Leona Harper gets into the car with Saul Levy? What about Parker and Maddie? Will they ever admit they're in love or are they destined to play this cat and mouse game forever?

Sign up for your **FREE** sneak peek at **DANCING SHOES**, the next installment of the Mt. Hope Adventure series at:

www.lynnegentry.com

Aren't the people of Mt. Hope fun? If you enjoyed escaping into the community of Mt. Hope, you'll be happy to know your adventure doesn't have to end with **SHOES TO FILL**.

The third book in the Mt. Hope Southern Adventures series, **DANCING SHOES**, is available. The final book, **BABY SHOES** is in the works. Sign up at **www.lynnegentry.com** if you'd like to be one of the first to know how to get your hands on the rest of the Mt. Hope Adventure series.

Enjoy this book? YOU can make a BIG difference.

Reviews are the most powerful tools in my arsenal when it comes to getting attention for my books. When loyal readers share their enthusiasm and their reviews on Amazon, it is secret gold to a book's ranking. I'm very grateful every time a reader tells their friends about this series and leaves a review on Amazon. I'm grateful for you, dear reader.

About the Author

Lynne Gentry knew marrying a preacher might change her plans. She didn't know how ministry would change her life. An author of numerous novels, short stories, and dramatic works, Lynne travels the country as a professional acting coach and inspirational speaker. Lynne's imagination loves to run wild. She also writes in the fantasy/science fiction genre of time travel. You can come along on the adventures she takes into historical worlds at **www.lynngentry.com**. Lynne lives in Dallas with her husband and medical therapy dog. She counts spending time with her two grown children and their families her greatest joy.

Let's connect on FaceBook @AuthorLynneGentry

Thanks for joining the Harper family on this leg of their Mt. Hope Adventure. I hope you'll take the next leg with Leona in DANCING SHOES, available at Amazon.

Free Sneak Peek Download

Find out what happens next in Mt. Hope …

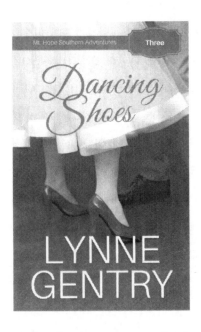

Subscribe to Lynne's **JOIN THE ADVENTURE** Newsletter.

Subscribers receive a FREE download of bonus material.

Find out how @:

www.lynnegentry.com

CPSIA information can be obtained
at www.ICGtesting.com
Printed in the USA
LVOW10s2052181217
560205LV00038B/2803/P